ANAMNESIS

Ages of Claya Book 1

Whitney H. Murphy

'Anamnesis'

When a new word,

just spoken,

is somehow familiar.

When a melody just learned

resonates with something ancient inside us.

When a voice

we've never heard

reaches our ears

and without understanding why,

we recognize it

as if we heard it once, long ago

in another time, another life—

When the New, in fact, in not new

but remembered.

Whitney H. Murphy

Before you go on . . .

There's something you must know, before you read further. The story that follows is a collection of memories. You may find the writing here to be strange, at first. Maybe less traditional or obvious than the stories you're accustomed to reading. In the beginning especially, you'll have questions. But this is natural, and the answers will come in time. As I'm sure you know, memories from long ago are never recalled all at once. And rarely with perfect clarity. This is a story of waking from sleep, of waking to one's identity. It must be told this way. As you read on, you will understand why.

—Lorëu

Prologue

In the beginning I have only dreams. They're shadowed and reeling in my mind, like thoughts born in tumbling waters, like shuddering leaves and slivers of lightning in the night. Sudden and strange, fogged and half-forgotten. Dreams. They terrify me—pull at my mind like a relentless wind, tearing me almost free of my small and dying body. And they leave me to wake with a start, heaving and trembling.

In the dreams I see things I can't explain. Beings with strange faces, smooth and pale and proud. Endless crowds of them—sometimes rushing, sometimes shuffling and turning about in their paths. I can't understand them. In the dreams I become something else—something whole and living, something ancient. I become a creature like the beings in the crowds, whose body knows how to live without struggle, never thinks of death. A creature from some other reality, like the lost memory of some old and faded lifetime. And it frightens me. But in time I begin to wait for the dreams. When waking brings short breath and an empty stomach, dreams begin to bring peace. Even the terrible ones.

1

I always wake with my voice stuck somewhere deep inside, buried and heavy like a stone in my chest. It's the same for us all, the longer we live.

A thin fog drapes over the ruins as morning comes, catching the sunlight and letting it out as a dim, yellow glow all around us. I blink the dew from my eyes and push slowly up onto my knees.

We've spent the last seven nights in the shadow of a fallen archway—the remnant of a city gate or broken sanctuary. No one knows for certain. There are many of them here, rising from the dark earth in random places, their stones cracked and colorless. These nights, as I've lain still in the darkness, I've heard them crumbling. Sinking.

I breathe. Thayl is already awake. He sits with his shoulders hunched over his knees at the edge of our shelter, looking silently out.

"She held on longer than most." He whispers without taking his eyes from the haze and broken stones in the distance. I crawl to kneel beside him, feeling cold.

"She was stronger than most," I breathe back. I struggle to pull my voice from its sleeping place. Somehow, the news doesn't shake me, not like I expected. My sister had fought the end with zeal— about as much as any frail and dying creature could hope to display. Just a day ago I found her climbing atop the heap of twisted spires that jut out from the rubble not far from our little camp. She was curling her little arms and legs around the narrow curves and pulling until she reached a shining, ball-tipped point. Watching her then, I wondered why she would waste the precious strength in her bones for such a senseless endeavor.

Now, I remember the way she looked as she grasped the pale stone—paused with her face raised to the sky, waiting. She must have seen something there. A bird or a cloud. She must have been exhausted.

In a way, I'm relieved to know her fight is over. But I don't look to the place where she lies. Not yet.

We dig a grave at the base of a broken tower nearby, not waiting for the others to wake. A shallow, rocky trench in the cool shade. It's the best we can do with our small and weary hands. Thayl finds a loose brick in the tower wall and heaves it out, then moves away as it tumbles out onto the ground. It kicks up little clouds of dirt and pebbles as it rolls, and I'm forced to squint the dust from my eyes. Together we position it over the grave, then remain crouching there, staring. I can't say why we do it, this odd ritual. But it feels right. We've done the same for all of them. Only twenty-three of us left now.

As struggling survivors in a ruined city, there are some things we never mention. Not because of any rule, but simply because they're realities that we can't hope to understand, can't dream of repairing. Realities we can't escape. Or forget. Like the truth that our bodies don't work anymore. We all know it—with every aching breath, we know it. Finding things to eat among the ruins is sometimes difficult, but even eating doesn't slow the end. Death bleeds us slowly, like a bitter poison crawling through our bones, our veins. We do our best to remember something like courage, but I can't help feeling like our bodies give up long before the battle begins. There's something missing, something we desperately need—no less than blood and breath. Something lost. But we can't name it. We're dying, like the sinking ruins all around us.

I've always supposed that my sister was somewhat older than me, although I never knew for certain. I hold my hand over her grave, fingers spread, dark palm to the sky, and wonder where they will bury me.

2

I had a mother once; I know I did. In the beginning, my sister and I would share our dreams and thoughts. Two daughters searching for the memory of Mother. But remembering our lives before the ruin of our land is like trying to recall the day before birth—hopeless, impossible. In many ways, it was a miracle that we somehow recognized one another. Most are fortunate to remember even their own names. I've often thought that I wouldn't have remembered mine if my sister hadn't called to me the instant we woke in those first dark hours. I can still recall the moment with every detail—the crushing weight of the stones pressing in against my lungs, the smell of dust and smoke and blood in my breath, the way my hands clutched and clawed instinctively at the rocks around my face.

"Lorëu!"

It was her voice. Somehow, I knew it. Évrieth, my sister. My sister's voice. And my name, Lorëu. Yes, that was always my name, wasn't it? My sister gave it back to me—found it like a dropped handkerchief in the rubble, along with my battered body.

We wandered in a daze through the cracked and dusted streets. Wandered for ages. It was two nights before we found Thayl, resting with his head tucked into his arms—almost hidden in the shadow of a collapsed, vine-blanketed house. His blackish color blended well with the darkness, despite being speckled with dirt and grease and mortar. And he was so calm, even then. Since those days, our little camp has never strayed far from the ruins. We've learned to find useful things among the rubble—food, clothing, tools, and shelter from the rain. We've learned to survive for nearly a month now, one dawn and dusk at a time.

I'm always wondering what sort of nation this land must have borne. What *our* nation must have been like. I've seen the bodies. We find them from time to time, lying in silent, crumbling places, sometimes clothed in brilliant colors, or adorned with shining rings and clasps and circlets. We must have been a prosperous people.

The wreckage of our land seems to go on forever. Once, when we had food to spare and the dust had settled somewhat, allowing the sunlight to fall in and warm the ground in places, I went searching. I followed the remnants of an old road, laying my steps between the weathered prints of wagon wheels in the dirt. I followed it through thickets and clearings, until the Old City fell behind and even the tallest of the ruined towers had sunken out of sight. In time I found myself at the bank of a wide and shallow river, crouching between the splintered remains of docks and boathouses. There are times when I think back to that moment, recalling the way the battered rafts and flatboats wobbled in the slow waves, still moored firmly in their places. Whatever happened to this land must have happened quickly. Before escape could even become an idea in our minds.

* * *

The day passes in fog. I move numbly through it, following like an odd shadow at Thayl's side as we scavenge for food.

When night returns, I dream of Évrieth climbing again along the twisted spires. She climbs with a sort of vigor I've never seen, as if she weighs nothing at all. And the orange sky frames and lights her little figure, makes her glow. She pauses at the top, only for a moment, before leaping to a lower spoke, white dress fanning out like a sail in her wake. I walk to the base of the spires, and she slides effortlessly down to meet me, smiling with a new kind of brilliance in her eyes. There's something different about the way she is, about the way she appears. Something more than strength and grace in her motion. But I can't explain it.

"Something's different," I tell her. "You're different, aren't you?"

Her smile remains, and she shakes her head softly, as if it were all too obvious. Maybe she knows something more.

"Don't forget, Lorëu," she tells me. "Don't forget what you are."

The stars are bright when the dream leaves me. *Beautiful.* All around, I can hear the soft sleeping breaths of the others. The sound of life. Alive together. Then somewhere in the distant night, I hear a wounded tower give way and collapse at last to the earth. And the sound of its fall rings out in all directions.

3

We can never remain idle for very long after someone leaves us. Loss has a way of tainting the air of a place, like bugs in the drinking water or fruit gone sour. It's become a sort of tradition after the burials to gather all we have—our meager supply of food, our salvaged clothing, our small array of tools and utensils—and set out in search of some new hideout in the ruins. In the past we've spent entire days shuffling along together, dividing into groups on occasion to search in every direction for a suitable campsite. But today we know our destination. Leading the way is Saiven—a tiny boy with bright eyes and a golden-brown speckle pattern that dots his head and back in uneven patches, like a poorly dyed garment. His feet scarcely meet the ground as he leaps and prances along—ragged tunic hanging off one shoulder. He throws back a glance with every few steps, assuring himself that his parade still follows. Kehlvi follows him more closely than any of us. She's a dust-colored girl who's looked after him since the beginning. They were together when they joined us.

I've long suspected that Saiven is the youngest of our group. He's certainly the smallest. Watching him now, I wonder how long he'll be able to display such an impressive amount of energy. He leads us northeastward through the more southern portion of the Old City, through several crumbling stone walls and onto a broad, paved lane where the colored bricks have risen and fallen in random places. I notice a number of the others pausing in the open space and pointing soundlessly down the length of the wide road. I stop to follow their gazes. This must have been one of the city's most lively avenues. It runs through the heart of the city, extending northward from our position for what looks to be a full day's walk until it reaches the hulking, sunken remains of what must have been a great Citadel. Much of the way is blackened beneath a great swathe of soot and feathery ash—gray dust that catches the breeze and stirs in little whirling motions along the scorched pavement. I shade my eyes and stare again at the Citadel where it lies, slumped like a hunched, dying beast at the end of the road. Somewhere near the center of its mass, a single spire still rises at an odd angle, pale and wavering in the midday heat.

A soft sensation of warmth comes to my arm as I look, and I become mildly aware that someone stands nearby. Thayl is staring too.

Saiven slips away shortly after we leave the Avenue, then reappears, leaping and wide eyed, clutching his prize in an outstretched hand. Something round and pinkish-yellow.

"*Gaik'eth!*" he squeals, motioning us onward. "Fruit! Trees and trees of them!"

We must have reached our destination. It lies just beyond a narrow opening in the slanted wall of a toppled structure. I stand back, waiting for the others to file through before crouching to follow close behind.

The gray earth that awaits us at the other side has caught the full brightness of the noonday sun, nearly blinding us as we come crawling out. I take a moment to squint. There's a kind of sweetness to the air here, and when I turn at last to take in the surrounding trees, which stand equally spaced and neatly aligned, I begin to feel an old word bubbling up in my throat. A word I had forgotten.

"Orchard."

I say it aloud. Saiven has found us an orchard. I step through the nearest row and pull a small, firm fruit from a branch looming over my head. All around, the others have already begun their feasting. They look so desperate, crouching in their worn, oversized shirts and tunics, scarcely pausing to breathe between greedy mouthfuls.

We end our meal after a short while for the sake of full stomachs—not weary of the fruits' wet, savory sweetness. Then we're all wandering curiously among the rows of leaves, peeking up and down the open dirt lanes that lie between them. It isn't long before we find a well at the southern end of the orchard. The old rope remains, hanging in a ragged coil from the well's narrow stone mouth. There are no buckets in sight, but we use the surviving metal clasp to lower our own pouches and chipped cups into the water below. It has an interesting taste, when we pull it up. Like dirt and cold stone and the summer wind all mingled together, with a subtle hint of ash. A spice from the distant Avenue. I sip it slowly and wonder how the orchard was spared from the flames and destruction that seem to have torn so much of the land. We'll likely never know. But with so much plenty, I feel my breath loosen. We'll be all right tonight, and perhaps for many nights to come. I never notice how anxious I am for our survival until something solid arises to reassure me—a wall between us and an otherwise more immediate death.

The afternoon comes calmly, bringing along a mild breeze. Most of the group has vanished into the ruins surrounding the orchard, searching for anything useful buried among the bricks and splintered wood. But I don't join them. There's a kind of stirring in my lungs that I can't settle. And the fruit has left me feeling unusually energized.

I wander southeastward until I find the orchard's far wall. It rises only to my nose. I press against it, lifting onto the tips of my feet to catch the view beyond. Is it a valley? The earth I glimpse seems to slope gradually away until it disappears from view altogether, perhaps descending to join with the more distant hills that come rolling in from afar. And it's all so *green*. Vibrant, alive. Something wild comes over me, and suddenly I'm searching for footholds as I climb awkwardly up and over the low stone wall. I overestimate my strength and come down on the other side with a jarring thump in the long grass, but I hardly notice. I rise to my feet and forget myself in the immensity of the view—endless emerald hills, spotted with great, billowing trees. Hills rippling out like bright waves from my position—out as far as I can gaze, until they meet with the sky at the sun's waking place, far away to the east. The wind is stronger here, and somehow different, in a way that rings like old singing to my ears. Like a song I once knew, or a name I once recognized. I teeter to remain balanced as it gusts musically from behind, then nearly stumble when it shifts and heaves against my side. The distant trees tremble in an excited dance, as if to encourage the sudden, violent play of the air. The tall grass whirls again along shimmering lines.

There's a massive stone not far from where I stand, rising at a slow angle from the hillside. I shuffle through the tall grass until I can place my palm to its cool face. I feel so fragile, so soft, beside the rock. If I were stronger, I'd climb atop. But my limbs are thin, and the wind steals my breath with its uneven gusts. I look to the clear sky. It's free of haze, and bluer than I've ever seen. There's a single white cloud, broken and sliding like a blade along the blue tones, slicing the sun and shifting toward the horizon. Watching, I expect to hear thunder as it meets the earth.

What is the sky? I watch it reaching on and on. Perhaps the sky is memory. Perhaps the sky is like an endless record, grasping all the scenes in my mind and rehearsing them over and over in its empty face. Maybe I could rediscover my memories there—remember who I am, if I looked closely enough. Perhaps the sky is time, or something beyond time. Why have I not noticed it before? I remain watching as the blue shades brighten with the returning presence of the sun, and then fade as if weary along the tips of the trees.

"There's an entire world out there, isn't there."

I hadn't heard him approach, but his voice doesn't startle me. I turn to see him standing several strides uphill, with his flat ears turned back against the wind in a way that makes him look almost angry. But I know he isn't.

"Do you think it happened everywhere, whatever happened here?" I ask him. Until I let it out, I don't realize how long the question has drifted in my mind. His eyes are full of thinking when he looks at me. He breathes.

"I don't know for certain," he says, "but I think this confusion ends somewhere. Somewhere far enough away to escape what happened here."

I give a slow nod. It feels right, what he's saying. We both look back to the hills. I close my eyes, just for an instant, listening. And I hear it again—that melody that hides itself in the way the wind whips and folds over the land. Like listening to an old poem. But the words are beyond my reach.

"Thayl," I speak without turning, "do you ever have a strange feeling like you're on the edge of a memory?"

"When you can almost remember something?" he asks.

I open my eyes, hand still flat against the stone beside me.

"The wind," I tell him. "Now and then, I can almost understand it, like someone's speaking just beyond my hearing."

Though the sounds of the steps behind me are carried away in the wind, I see his shadow line up beside my own. His dark hand settles gently atop my shoulder. And when I turn, I can see the rolling hills in his pupils.

"Keep listening," he says.

4

My dreams begin to change after we move to the orchard. The strange crowds I've so often seen are gone, and instead I'm left wandering alone through mist and shade. Sight comes to me in random flashes as I shuffle along, and I struggle to make any sense of the fleeting light, the scattered darkness. Somewhere in the midst of the visions I often hold my hands before me and try to focus on them, willing my eyes to stay open. But they look different when I see them. At first, I can't name it. They're just *different*. But when the dream comes to me for the fourth time, I finally recognize why. This time, I open my eyes to find that my hands are pale—frighteningly pale—and naked, like the little worms I've seen in dirt. Naked, hands and arms alike. What *am* I? What have I become—?

This time, the dream throws me back into the orchard with a start, and I find myself raising an arm instinctively for inspection. But my arm remains as it always has been, clothed in soft, earth-colored fur, like the rest of my body. I let my breath ease out. Just a dream.

* * *

Five days after our move, we have another burial. It's odd how a little food can make us forget about death for a time. But now it comes like a sudden impact to my mind, tossing me back into the reality of our survival. This time it's Iredehl. A strong, gray-eyed boy with fur the color of sunset—orange and red and yellow in places. The last I would expect to find lying cold and motionless beside the well when morning comes. It wasn't hunger that took him. *Iredehl*. They named him for the colors in his fur. He never did remember his true name.

We bury him farther away than usual, carrying his carefully wrapped body back to the Avenue and southward, until the ruined city ends and the trees begin. We leave him there, near the roots of a towering tree, at the gate of the woods. Maybe it's an attempt to keep death away from our new camp—a place too fortunate to leave behind. For now.

* * *

Another two days pass before we begin to think about practical things again. We learned long ago to make small fires for light and warmth at night, using only a certain kind of black, porous stone and a handful of dry wood splinters for kindling. It's our habit to carry the stones with us as we wander from place to place. But they're softer than most, and in time they whittle away until they're little more than brittle crumbles in our pockets. Now we're down to only one and a half. I wonder how we managed to become so careless.

There's a place not far from my sister's grave— where we once camped for a short time, near the western edge of the ruins—where we've always been able to find the firestones. They lie in piles there, spilled out from splintered barrels under a torn and toppled awning. Thayl volunteers to go. Kehlvi and I join him.

From the orchard, the journey takes several hours. It's late afternoon when we come to the western ruins with the sun in our eyes, three of us together. I feel a subtle flutter in my chest as the fallen arches come into view—dark, hulking shapes, outlined in the orange light of the sinking sun. A place where my sister once walked. I look ahead and find Thayl glancing back at me. Maybe he feels it too.

We have only one sack for gathering the firestones. A broad pouch only slightly larger than the leather vessels we use for water. Kehlvi crouches and holds the sack open as we crawl under the fallen roof behind the awning and pull out the stones in little handfuls. It takes no time at all. Thayl ties the sack and loops it over his shoulder when it's filled. We're ready to start back. I rise to my feet.

And then I feel it—a solid, sinking sensation in my stomach. It rises along my spine and rattles my breath, grabbing at my heart. Like a cold wave springing up out of nothing to splash over my shoulders. Something isn't right. I look up at Thayl and open my mouth to say something, *anything*, but my voice doesn't come. Can't they feel it? Kehlvi has just noticed my expression and is beginning to let a puzzled look fall over her face when she's jerked abruptly and violently forward to the ground before her—a massive, pointed shaft piercing her through the middle and forcing a sudden, terrible cry from her chest.

For a moment—an eternity—I'm too shocked to move, too stunned to breathe or scream. I can only stand motionless, wide eyes fixed upon the great spear point where it has lodged itself, extending like a great wet spire from the flesh. Kehlvi's flesh. Then Thayl grips my arm—and I'm moving as quickly as my bones can manage, stooping to take Kehlvi's left arm over my shoulder and lift her from the dirt. Thayl takes the right side, and together we stumble around the nearest arch and over a heap of bricks, heading back east. Gasping. I wish we could run, but our feet can scarcely manage a panicked shuffle. We move as rapidly as we can— Kehlvi struggling to move her feet enough to ease our way, hot blood running in little rivers down her front and sides and splattering her legs. But she only wheezes softly. I marvel at her strength. The spear tips and bobs with every motion of her body, still lodged firmly in place.

"Did you see it?" Thayl huffs as we struggle onward.

"See what?" I choke back, tears suddenly swelling out and raining down my face.

"The thing that threw the spear."

I'm starting to cough on my own breaths.

"You *saw* it?" I gasp. He gives only a trembling, tight-jawed nod in reply, looking ahead. And he says nothing more. We move for the orchard. Our path through the ruins is tortured and endless. I can feel Kehlvi's strength bleeding out onto the earth as we go, and I wonder if she'll live to see the others. To see Saiven.

The Avenue is dark when we reach it. We start to yell and shout, desperately hoping the others will hear.

"Ak'yal! Ak'yal! Savusyat'!"

But our voices echo alone back to our ears. How can they not hear us? We've come almost to the western edge of our camp, the orchard wall in sight. But there's no firelight, no sound. My stomach plunges a second time, and I try to jerk the other two instinctively northward, away from the campsite.

"We can't go there. Come on," I whimper to them. "We can't go in there. Something's wrong."

"We've got to get out of sight, underneath somethi—" Thayl begins, then falls abruptly silent mid-sentence, looking over his shoulder. This time I see it too—standing motionless by the western side of the road, not far south of our position. It's *huge*, with two legs, two arms, and a head, like us—only *massive*. The darkness of the night conceals its features. But I don't mind. I don't care to see.

Fear and dire need do something remarkable to our frail bodies. We're scrambling near the middle of the wide Avenue, entirely helpless, weary and terrified. But before I can turn away from the awful Creature down the road, Thayl has stooped down and lifted Kehlvi—thick spear and all—completely off the ground, and is hobbling as fast as his worn feet can possibly bear him. I follow breathlessly behind. We climb over the rubble and continue on a northeastern path, until we've left the orchard far behind us. The monster *must* have seen us. But it doesn't follow.

"*T'ot'avan*, this way!"

The voice is small, urgent. We follow the sound, and come to a place where a little structure lies hidden between several larger remains. It's collapsed only partly, creating a dark hollow below its slanted wall. We duck beneath it without looking back. A handful of the others are hiding in the shadows there, eyes round as the moons outside. Saiven is with them, and he yelps and wails softly as we lay Kehlvi carefully down on her side. She can barely manage a soft sigh when her eyes find the little boy. At least she can see him, before the end.

No one asks what happened. We use our old shawls and tunics to make her as comfortable as we can, supporting the weight of the shaft with a brick to ease the torque on her side. Then Thayl and I back away, letting the others hold and surround her in her last moments. We move to the cold wall and shut our eyes against the darkness, the terror of the night, the memory of the Creature by the road. I crawl into Thayl's trembling arms and he holds me tightly to his heart. And I fall asleep to the sound of its beating.

5

The sun finds subtle ways to slip into our shelter when morning comes again, falling in like little ribbons and highlighting the dust in the cool air. Kehlvi left us sometime in the night. Someone has already made a simple veil from the end of a shawl for her eyes, and laid her slender hands together on the dirt before her. Little Saiven lies curled at her feet, still asleep.

I sit slowly upright and gaze around the shelter. There are eight of us huddled here together. Eight, out of the twenty-two who were gathered yesterday. Thirteen others may or may not be alive. I wonder where else they might have fled. Thayl stirs softly beside me, then sits up, dusty and weary eyed. We sit soundlessly for a moment, letting the situation settle slowly into our minds. I look down at my arms and hands, at the way Kehlvi's blood has caked my brown fur and dried it into clumps. Now that I see it, the smell in the air becomes suddenly obvious. A heavy, almost metallic scent. I've seen more death than I care to think about. It's a part of our lives, however undesired it may be. But death has never involved this—not blood, not terrible pain and fear. Death used to be something peaceful.

After a time, Thayl sighs and holds up his own arm, as if to compare.

"We should wash this off," he says.

We're not sure how to move when we leave the hideout. We travel slowly, glancing all around, watching our steps. In time we come creeping to the northern wall of the orchard with our hearts throbbing in our chests. It wasn't long ago that I had enough strength to pull myself over the low stones. But today is different. My arms and legs ache from their exertion the night before. So weak. So frail. Today, I have no strength. No strength to climb, no strength to escape the spear-throwing monster, if it appears again. And as we creep along, the reality of our frailty—our *helplessness*—weighs suddenly down like a crushing boulder on my mind. Heavy—pinning me to the earth like the ruined bricks that trapped me in my first waking moments. Our bodies are dying. Giving up before life can begin. But it wasn't always this way, was it?

I slip my hands into the cracks and crevices of the wall as I wonder, preparing to climb.

Was it?

A strange sensation comes into my mind, like the haziness before a dream. Subtle at first, but it grows. And then I'm caught away—suddenly elsewhere, running. Running down a narrow lane with my colored dress waving and flapping around my knees. I hear the clapping of my brown sandals along the pavement, recognize the soft swat of my long hair against my shoulders. Long, earth-colored curls. And there's someone waiting there, at the end of the lane.

Then the dream pulls away like a veil from my eyes, and I find myself clinging partway up the orchard wall.

A dream? Or something else?

Thayl helps me over the wall by pushing from behind, and in a moment I come toppling over the other side with a gasp at my teeth. I roll limply to a stop with my face to the sky, not caring if any monster may have heard. I need to find my breath again.

* * *

We eat our fill of fruit before continuing onward, watching and listening to the sounds of the morning. Aside from a mild breeze and the subtle crumbling of the dirt beneath our feet, there's nothing. We travel the length of the orchard, moving toward the south and keeping the Avenue in sight all the while. And when the trees begin, I decide to lead Thayl along the old road. We pass Iredehl's fresh grave as we enter the woods, ducking instinctively through the leaves to hide ourselves. It seems like it was months ago when we buried him.

The river is wider and slower toward its northern end. We come to the low bank well upstream of the ruined boathouses and scan the opposite shore. Nothing but the slow sway of the trees and the flitting of birds. Thayl wades in first, sloshing almost to the center of the flow where the cold water rolls and creases like silk around his waist. He leans against the gentle surge as he bends to lower his dark arms beneath the surface. The water is clean—rushing and clear. As I step from the bank, I can see the colored stones lying below. And my dark silhouette. I watch it ripple and shimmer as I go, staring at the crown. No long curls hang there— only the outline of the same soft, short fur that clothes my entire body. As it ought to. I shake my head. Such odd dreams I have.

I wade into the flow until the river reaches my lower back and pause, turning to face upstream.

Energy. . . .

The thought comes softly to my mind, rising from the rushing stream.

Energy. The energy of life. The force of the water, the life of the trees. The birds have it; the wind has it. The energy of life within all things.

The river is singing. I listen to its voice, and for a moment I forget my pains, my weariness, my fear. It's a melody I've heard before but couldn't understand.

Until now. Strength is energy. And suddenly, I'm thirsting for it. All over, thirsting for it. I close my eyes and feel the thirst burning in my body—coiling up my spine and buzzing in my fingertips. *Thirsty.* Without thinking, I plunge beneath the face of the stream and let the current slide over me, hands clinging to the smooth rocks at my chest. The river has power.

Will you help me find it? I speak back to the rushing voice, then open my eyes, squinting against the surge. There are fish—clouds of tiny fins and eyes, quivering to remain in the shadow of rocks. And larger ones, with flat tails swaying softly behind them. Energy. The fish have it too. Something startles them as I watch, and in an instant the scene is alive with motion— slender, shining bodies darting in every direction. Overcome by some wild instinct, I thrust out my hands with all my might and bring my palms together in the midst of the cloud. Something writhes and wiggles there against my skin. *Energy!* I open my heart to the thirst and let the tension release along my spine, my arms, my hands. It opens my veins in a sudden pulse, pulling like sharp lightning at the thing between my palms and tearing the power from the slender muscle there.

It only takes an instant. Then I'm standing, the river running like rain from my chin and elbows, staring at the limp fish clutched in my hands. Somewhere nearby, I hear Thayl gasp.

I should be thrilled to have caught myself a little meal, but the meat matters little to me now. I tip my catch into one hand to free the other, curling and stretching my fingers, suddenly too astonished to think anything at all.

6

"Tell me again how you did it." He leans toward me as he speaks, wide eyes deep and hungry. We're sitting in the grass beside the massive boulder, at the edge of the eastern hills we found beyond the orchard. I wanted to hear the wind again.

I bite my lip and look out at the scene.

"I'm not sure how else to describe it," I tell him. "It was like . . . opening something inside. Or . . . listening to something natural inside me. Somehow, the fish's energy became my own."

Thayl is gazing thoughtfully at his own palm when I turn back.

"Natural." He repeats it softly to himself, then gives me a curious look, chin tilting downward. "Teach me how to do it."

The wind whips a sudden swirl through the grass, stirring the tall blades and making them tickle our necks.

"*Teach* you?" I swat the grass away from my head. "It was only by some miracle of luck that I caught the fish. How could we ever hope to snatch another?" He holds his hand up like an offering between us.

"Do it to me," he says. I feel my eyes widen.

"What if it hurts you?" I don't like the idea. But even as I use my own hand to lower his, I can't help but notice the energy that resonates there. Vibrant, like a coil under pressure. Thayl must have seen the moment on my face. He presses his case.

"Just try it. You can always let go, right?"

"What good would it do?" I ask him, feeling suddenly tense all over.

"Jog our memory, I hope," he says, and he braces against the earth with his other hand. I lay my palm flat on his arm, gripping firmly. *Breathe.* I can always let go.

This time, I have more control. I feel the energy at my fingertips, and it becomes tangible, *movable.* Like it should be—like it should've been all along. Somehow, my bones know it. It's an effortless act. I pull the strength from the muscle before me and make it my own. It flows as a warm surge into my wrist, my forearm. A wonderful, healing sensation. But only for one of us. Thayl's hand falls limp almost immediately, and I see his jaw tighten as his shoulder writhes impulsively away. The sun returns from behind a cloud as I let go, pouring its yellow light onto the hillside. It falls into Thayl's dark fur and highlights the hidden gray and amber tones there. My palm is buzzing.

"I hurt you," I say. But he shakes his head.

"No, you've just made my arm very tired," he breathes, "very suddenly."

I lean toward him.

"Did you feel the way it flows?" I take his weakened hand and place it on my own upturned arm. "Can you feel it?" We sit in silence for a moment, and I notice my heart racing. We're about to discover something wonderful. I *know* it. Thayl concentrates, staring directly at me. But his focus is elsewhere—the way a gaze shifts when a distant dream or buried thought comes unexpectedly to mind. I wait for a time, testing the strength in my arm, sliding and shifting it along the muscle, the tendon. It moves like warm static beneath my skin. I look back to my friend.

"Take it back," I tell him. He nods, and his grip becomes suddenly firm. It startles me when he pulls the strength away. My arm is swallowed in sudden fatigue—

a fatigue which turns from a dull ache to acid-like burning before I can react. And when he takes his hand away, my arm is left feeling as if it had just borne some massive weight—every speck of energy exhausted, every muscle aflame. He took it back. I can't suppress an excited laugh. Thayl opens and closes his thin fingers, testing the new strength.

"It worked," he says, and a wild smirk spreads over his face. And I can see the fire churning in his eyes.

That night, I don't sleep. Dawn is creeping along the horizon before my excitement can settle. I forget about my fears and come out under the pale light, wandering in circles with my hands to the sky. I watch the stars in their fading moments, feel the chilling sigh of the night as it dies in the west. We've begun to remember something—something good, something sorely needed. And I can feel it pushing a strange sensation into my heart. A feeling like the light that comes spreading over the hills now, or like warm wind on a blustery day. A feeling I'm almost reluctant to accept at first. I pause atop the thick remains of a fallen wall, watching a little cloud of birds as it passes along the yellowing sky. The sound of my heart swells at the sight of it, resonating to my knees, my feet, my fingertips. And at last a name for the sensation rises softly in my ears. Is it *hope*?

7

We took all morning to reach this place. It's at the center of the ruined city, where some thick walls and rooftops still stand, shaken but not toppled. The opening in the wall before us is wide—gaping like a great, yawning mouth in the Citadel's eastern remains. It's tall enough to be seen from halfway down the Avenue. I pause near the heap of broken blue and red tiles that pour from its jaws and look up into the shadowed space beyond, wondering what force might have torn so easily through the massive bricks.

It was Thayl's idea to come here. We practiced our newfound skill for days, stealing energy back and forth, taking more every time, taking it faster. We learned to use the whole length of our arms in the process, rather than the palms only. We made it a new reflex, a memory in our bones. A memory we've awakened.

And we began to teach the others. After three nights we were sharing strength throughout our entire company. Together, we began to discover wonderful things. For the first time in my waking life, I could *run*. It was a remarkable feeling, to throw my legs out, to feel the welcoming impact of the earth beneath my feet, the air rising like a dry wave at my face. Breath heaving, heart soaring. One step, and another. I could take three fast strides—three quick steps in a row before the fatigue came crawling along my knees and forced me to stop, gasping but exhilarated. The thrill of it burst and crackled like lightning in my veins, a wild sensation unlike any I had experienced before. What a miracle they became to me, these skinny legs.

I was still entranced with the idea of running when Thayl brought his thoughts to me that evening. It was in the strangest hour of the night when I heard him whisper. That time when the world is silent but not sleeping, when we lie at the edge of the day's memory, watching the scenes of life flash and flicker meaninglessly in our eyes. I'd lain sleepless for ages.

"Lorëu."

Soft, yet sure. He knew I was awake. I rose on one elbow, twisting to look over my shoulder. He was lying on his back an arm's length away, hands resting loosely on his stomach. It was a warm night. No need to curl up.

For a time, we said nothing, and I could hear the wind playing along the cracked bricks near our heads, attempting to join us.

"I saw something," he said to the slanted roof of our shelter, "when you first taught me to move energy."

"What did you see?" I asked. Was that dread in his eyes? He turned to me without blinking, and his voice was flat when it came.

"I saw the Citadel."

The next sunrise found us almost halfway along the northern length of the Avenue. Now, at the peak of the day, we stand shielding our eyes against the glare that leaps from the massive marble and granite walls of the city's center. The entrance we've found is broad enough for six of us to stand together, shoulders aligned. Thayl takes the strength of my arm to climb up the sliding tiles and pull himself into the jagged opening, then lies flat on his stomach and extends his own hand for me to grasp. I take back only enough energy to find a firm grip on the stones, using footholds and Thayl's help to do the rest. Then we sit for a time just within the entrance, letting breath return.

I glance around. We sit at the edge of a broad, curving hallway. It stretches on for only a few strides in both directions before vanishing behind its own curve. Our arrival has excited a little cloud of dust, and I watch as it floats and settles over us. The floor is dark and smooth, blanketed with a layer of powder—a faint, grayish veil along the cool surface, disturbed in places where bits of rubble have tumbled loose and shattered—leaving thin streaks that radiate out in random directions. There's something here—in the stale air, in the firmness of the stone walls—something lingering that hints at immensity. Without seeing any farther beyond these dark walls I can already sense it. This place was once very grand.

We rise and take the passage to our left, blinking sun blotches from our eyes when the shadows close in. Our steps are the only sound, echoing calmly along the polished walls as we move along. We follow the northward curve of the path. In time, the outer wall opens in a series of arched windows. They rise almost to the vaulted ceiling, allowing the midday sun to pour in over the tiled floor and splash against the inner wall. I squint uncontrollably as we pass. Then the corridor abruptly ends, merging into a shadowed space with an arched entrance. We come to a stop at the threshold and stare dumbfounded into the space beyond. I fail to catch my breath before it slips away.

Only several steps ahead, the walls curve and sweep away from our position, and the already-towering ceiling rises sharply to a breathtaking height—great columns rising like ancient trees to support it. The domed roof sits high atop a neck of slotted windows, allowing a gentle glow to fall in and light the great Hall before us. We shuffle slowly into the immense, circular center, turning round and round over the brilliantly colored floor, struggling to capture the sight of it all. I find my jaw hanging somewhere below its usual place and pull it up, managing a half-whisper.

"What . . . *was* this place?"

Thayl is already moving toward one of the three massive stairways that lead away from the Hall in different directions. He pauses at the first step, looking up.

"Maybe we'll remember, eventually." His voice echoes back, continuing past my ears and hiccupping along the walls and dusty columns, rising up into the towering dome. I suppress a stiff shudder. This place isn't empty. I can smell the stale breath of old memories here, shifting and crawling like smoke all around us. People walked here. Crowds of them. Not so long ago. They've gone away, but they left their memory here. It sticks like old perfume in the air. It's a bitter taste on my tongue, and now that I've breathed it in, I can't stop noticing.

I follow Thayl up the polished steps. Another broad passage leads away from the upper landing, lined with openings on either side and ending with a pair of giant double doors. *Doors.* It's a concept that strikes me. One I had forgotten. The idea of a barrier that closes us away from whatever lies beyond. A seal to keep the world out. Or to hide behind. Doors were once a very ordinary thing to me, I suppose.

Curiosity draws us apart. I turn into the first opening at my left and find that the next three all lead into the same chamber. It's a long rectangular room, filled with a tousled array of items that are all at once overwhelmingly familiar to me. Carved, thin-legged chairs; tables with worn, dusty tablets scattered over them; and tall shelves struggling to keep the last of their rolled records from tumbling out onto the floor.

Records, words, writing. I can read, can't I? How had I forgotten about books? I cross to the nearest shelf and pull a scroll from its place, inspecting the seal.

Ts'ufi Yet'a Division, Movements of the Seventy-Eighth Year.

I *can* read. But the jagged letters are strange and old to me. Reading them wrinkles my thoughts and presses against some distant place in my mind— reworking some muscle that has slept for ages. And the words make no sense. There's a certain tension at my fingertips. I reach for another scroll.

Record of the Seventy-Second Year, Ts'ufi Ataran.

Ataran. . . . The seal is pressed smooth, glossed over with some sort of waxy glue.

"*Ts'ufi Ataran.*" I read it aloud, and the last word sets something ringing at the edge of my mind.

Ataran. . . .

I don't notice my slow, backward shuffle until a chair nudges gently against my legs, and I plop clumsily down onto the hard seat. A *large*, hard seat. Even with my weight at the edge of the chair, my feet can scarcely brush the floor. I raise my head and glance again at the furniture that fills the soundless room. How had I not noticed its size until now? Whatever people spent their days in this chamber must have been tall. And big.

The silence of the room is strange. I sit for a time and try to listen, but the memories that dwell here are becoming somehow unsettling. I can't stay. Sliding from the chair, I turn back out into the broad hallway and wander down its length—passing rooms and rooms full of all the same things. Tables, chairs, shelves, and carved drawers. All unbroken. I look at them, and the memory of the splintered docks along the river flashes faintly in my mind. How is it that scrolls and tablets lie almost undisturbed in this place? Lightly tossed—while all the city has collapsed around it?

I spot Thayl standing motionless at the far side of a small chamber near the corridor's end, staring away from me. For an instant I'm fooled, and there's someone else—another person standing there, staring back at Thayl with a loose slant in his shoulders and an all-too-familiar gleam in his dark eyes. But I blink and stare again to see only Thayl—and a mirror that rises from the floor to the painted ceiling.

Mirror, yes . . . that thing that shows . . .

Thayl hears me at the doorway and turns, motioning with his hand.

"Come and see," he tells me. "It's strange, isn't it?"

I step into the room. For an odd moment, I hesitate. Like seeing my clear reflection will somehow change me—take my waking reality and turn it into something else, something I can't expect. But it's a senseless fear. I step toward the silvery reflection. It's plenty large enough to frame us both.

And there I am. Thin and frail, staring back at myself with gaping brown eyes that match my soft, short fur. It's the same color that covers my entire body, hidden only in part by the loose, ragged tunic that hangs on me like a blanket on a drying line. We've never needed much clothing, with our dense fur. But we feel strange without it.

There are the features I can expect. The large eyes and flat nose, the wide ears that hang flat and smoothed against the sides of my head, and the thin mouth with pointed teeth that poke occasionally into view. These are the features I've always seen in the people who surround me. But this time, it's me. *Lorëu.*

I must have looked into mirrors before—before everything that's happened here, when the world was as it should be, when we lived whatever lives we had. But looking now, I begin to wonder just how long we've struggled. Why do I have this odd sensation in my throat? Staring into the glassy image, I almost can't recognize myself. But it *is* me. I step closer and peer into my own eyes, watching the shining wetness there. These are the same eyes, the same hands. This is the same little body that woke beneath the rubble that day, when Évrieth found it, the first day of my memory. We've managed to survive a few things together, this little body and me.

I've never noticed my size before. Standing beside me in the mirror, Thayl's taller figure seems to dwarf my own. Maybe he heard my thought. He raises his hand and draws a line in the air, marking the difference in our heights, smirking softly. I allow myself a laugh, and watch as the brown girl in the mirror shows her pale teeth.

* * *

The double doors at the end of the corridor are immense—held in place by six massive, shining hinges and painted the color of old blood. Brownish red, dusty. Even Thayl's head stands just below the height of the bronzy handles. It takes several minutes of our best efforts to crack one door open. A soft breath of wind escapes through the threshold and rolls over my arm as we do so. It smells different than the air in the rooms we're coming from. *Feels* different. We heave the door only enough to make a small gap—just enough to slip through and into the space beyond. Thayl slides through first. He stands barely inside, at the very edge of the new room, turning to look all around. There's more sunlight beyond the doors. It beams past him and plays in stripes along the floor at my feet, fleeing back into the corridor behind me. It's a pleasant shining.

But for some reason I can't name, my heart is beginning to throb—like all the faded memories of this place are pressing at my back, threatening to jab or pinch at any moment. I can't stay out here alone. I'm turning my shoulders to fit through the tight opening along the door's edge when Thayl looks back to me.

"I just remembered something," he says. "I think this place wa—"

It's strange, the way time slows to silence, the way motion becomes a half-frozen dream—predictable yet irreversible—when something terrible suddenly catches you. I see Thayl's gaze turn away from me, directed somewhere beyond my sight. The gleam falls from his eyes, and I see a kind of horror rising and flooding the dark circles there. For an instant. And then he is gone. Knocked backward, pulled or shoved—I can't tell. Gone with nothing more than a low gasp. I press through the door in a frantic scramble, throwing back the urge that screams through my nerves, commanding me to run back—back through the dome and curving hall, out and away from this dying place.

I glance around the new room only enough to recognize its tremendous size. I see no beast, no towering monster. Only Thayl, holding his head and writhing on the elaborately tiled floor, gasping and choking terribly.

Now I feel it, the presence in this room. It's thick, heavy, *stifling*. It floods the room like black smoke, withering thought and blacking out the light—though the sunlight still peers brightly in all around us. For a moment I wonder if I can survive it at all. But it isn't concentrated on me.

Thayl!

I rush to his side and take hold of his thrashing shoulders. The terror is searing—sharp and cold in my throbbing heart.

Thayl!

I link my arm under his and try to pull him away, away from the blackness and horror here. But he trembles too violently to support the effort, and I topple backward onto the floor. There's death here, lurking in the walls, the floor, the arched ceiling. I feel it watching, waiting.

"No!" I scream, tears suddenly bursting out and blurring my sight. I crawl back and wrench Thayl's tensed and clawing hand into my own, turning to the concentrated presence that lurches ruthlessly over him. It takes no notice of me. I shout again, and something cracks inside me—like the firestones when they strike—and I'm suddenly aflame.

"*GET OUT!*" My voice shrieks almost too loud for my own ears to register, and I find myself standing, jaw clenched, hand outstretched and pointing to the heart of the black presence . . . or to the place where it *was*. Suddenly, I can no longer sense it. Then the flame in my chest subsides as quickly as it erupted. I'm still lowering my hand, wondering stupidly at what I've done, at the rage that came over me, when Thayl climbs to his feet and jerks at my arm.

"We need to go. *Now*," he breathes. I notice the great red door as I turn to follow him. When did it fall shut again?

The entryway where we stand opens into a wide corridor, where the light of many towering windows lies in stretched, faded shapes across the floor. We hurry along it as quickly as we can manage, sharing strength back and forth to keep up our speed as we go. The memory of running taunts and flutters at the edge of my mind all the while. I wish so dearly to run.

The circular room at the end of the passage offers no obvious escape. It stands empty, occupied only by a massive dark-wood desk and matching hulking chair. The place is encircled with a kind of raised colonnade. The pillars begin several reaches above the height of our heads and rise to the roof above, where they're overshadowed by the dramatically overhanging eaves. Although grand, this was a private place. I can feel it.

"We can use the desk," I say, gesturing to the low wall beneath the columns, "or the chair."

Thayl nods in reply, and we hurry to the chair at the center of the room. For some reason we try to lift it first, pressing our shoulders to the undersides of the thick arms. It only takes a moment for a better plan to evolve, and then we're heaving and pulling the massive chair toward the northern wall.

Escape, escape. . . .

I struggle to think of anything else. We're only a few pulls from the wall when I sense the darkness again—it seeps like subtle smoke at first, gliding soundlessly.

"It's coming back," I whisper, failing to hide the tremor in my voice. From across the seat of the chair, Thayl throws a glance around the room.

"Almost there. Just keep pushing," he tells me. Another heave, another handful of steps toward the wall. Now only a shoulder's width away.

"That's good enough—get up there, Lorëu!" Thayl almost shouts, and I move with a start. I scramble onto the broad seat of the chair, then up onto the thick arm. The tips of my fingers can only play at the top of the wall, and I search frantically for a foothold on the tall back of the chair. Presence fills the room behind me, and a silent horror comes gripping along my spine that I'm hopeless to dispel. My hands tremble uncontrollably against the stone.

"You can make it!" Thayl shouts desperately from behind, climbing atop the chair and pressing his hands to my back, as if he were about to give me a push. But he doesn't push. He does something else. There's an explosion where his palms rest—hot and electric, bursting through my back in a searing wave and rippling out into my limbs. I coil naturally in response, and find myself leaping from the chair with more force than I ever knew my little body could produce. Echoes ring out through the columns as I jump—a terrible pounding, and the sharp snap of splintering wood. My leap easily clears the wall. I tuck my knees to my chest and fly between the columns, pivoting as I go and straining to catch a fleeting glimpse of the scene behind. It flashes by—a shattered desk, Thayl rising to his feet, and something else—

And then the wall rises between us.

I hadn't considered my landing. The earth outside the wall is farther down than I expect, sloping away and blanketed with weeds. By some miraculous chance I land on my hands and feet, facing uphill, then tumble backward for what seems like ages. Sky, dirt, and sky again. The world whirls and heaves all around me. When it flattens, I come to a stop with limbs scratched and throbbing all over. And for a moment I'm motionless in the dirt, staring blankly up at the afternoon sky. Such vibrant blue! The clouds roll like spreading leaves across the azure face above.

Thayl!

I want to run, to leap and fly—to climb back to the Citadel and somehow into the columned room again, to find a way to save my friend. But I can't run, and instead I lie in the weeds, aching everywhere. What happened to us, just now?

A footfall sounds and shakes me from my thoughts. It's solid and heavy, not like any sound my people would make as they move. But undoubtedly a footstep. I lift my head to glance wearily over my shoulder. The sight of the figure I see there startles my heart into leaping. The Creature is just as tall as I remember it. And this time, there's no darkness to shroud its massive shape. It stands entirely clothed in swathes of faded green clothing that are wrapped and tied snugly around its thick figure. Only the eyes remain uncovered, peering down at me from the shaded security of a head wrap. Little eyes, black eyes. They blink only once when I turn and see them. It holds a knife.

I turn away and crawl to my feet, try to run. But the Creature closes in with two rumbling strides before I can find my balance. A broad arm appears across my shoulders and jerks me backward, sweeping me entirely off the ground. There's no chance for thought, no chance to plan. There's only the struggle—and so little time to give it.

But I don't need time, I tell myself. I only need a firm grip.

Heart in my throat, I cling to the massive arm as it pulls me backward. There's such strength there, so much swelling energy! Power greater than any I've felt in the frail arms of my people. And now it's mine. The clothing doesn't slow me down as much as I expect. I pull the Creature's strength without holding back. A weighty gasp comes to my ears, and the strong pull of my captor's arm falls instantly loose. I wiggle free and drop to the earth, hands tingling with the hot surge of new energy. Then the monster lashes out again with its other arm, swinging the dagger at my head. I flinch and stumble away, hoping to run. But my legs are knocked out from beneath me before I can try. I tumble forward and land on my hands—dirt and rocks biting at my fingers. Then the Creature is crouching over me in what may be an attempt to scoop me up in its one good arm. But I interrupt the motion. I press my arms and hands to its massive chest and focus all my effort. I feel for the energy churning there—the tensed muscle, the open lungs, the great throbbing heart—and I take it all. I let my limbs open to the surge, let the strength pour like fluid fire into my shoulders, my head, my spine. It drains until I'm entirely overwhelmed, until the giant lungs grow still and the heart becomes nothing more than a faint, irregular flutter against my palm. And then it's over. The monster hunches over and collapses headfirst into the ground, dull eyed and lifeless. I scramble out of the way and climb to my feet, trembling terribly.

Thayl!

I spin around until I spot the tall Citadel, the columned room at the top of the rocky hill, and begin stumbling toward it. But the newly stolen strength is almost more than my little body can bear. The world grows suddenly hot and bright all around me, and I struggle to see the white columns in the distance. Dizziness swirls like a storm into my mind. My knees begin to quiver and wobble awkwardly with each step. The Citadel isn't far, only up the slope, only a few paces away. . . .

But now my consciousness slumps—hangs heavily on thin thread at the edge of my mind. When it falls, I'm hopeless to catch it. And the white gleam of the afternoon sun along the walls of the Citadel is the last sight to reach my weary eyes.

8

He's still a young man when he comes to the House of Voices, stepping with slow, lengthy strides along the white pavement, colorful robes draped in thick folds over his shoulders. Even as a young man, he bears a stern and noble demeanor—the kind of bold presence rarely carried by even the highest officers of the Voice.

There are tales in the streets these days. Whispers and rumors that spark up excitedly in his wake wherever he walks, rising like thin seeds on the breeze and drifting into every alley of the city. They say he's noble born—the last of the old line of kings long ago deposed. They say the gods have raised themselves a new Hand to direct the Voice. They say he's magnificent.

The whispers long ago drifted into the vaulted halls of the House. But the leaders of the people never heed the senseless superstitions of the streets. Or so they are taught.

"Do you think he's all they say he is, Father?"

The son of the Eviskyóneh stands staring down at the newcomer from the edge of the southern balcony, just beyond his father's shadow. Somehow, watching the young new officer of the Voice march silently to the southern entrance sends a kind of twisting through his stomach. He shivers unconsciously, pulling at the silk sleeves of his tunic.

But his father remains calm and expressionless, fine lines beneath his eyes accenting the weariness in his face. The weariness he's always trying to hide—to pack away at the back of his mind with all the other unimportant issues of daily life. But his son can still see it.

"We'll see," he murmurs to the boy after a time, not taking his gaze from the columns below. "We'll see."

9

We can't find her. Streets and alleyways, narrow lanes—winding, endless cobbled paths before us, all flooded with figures. Running, stumbling, terrified. And the darkness is stifling. It lies thick on our eyes and sticks like cold silt on our skin. Cold, and suffocating.

We can't find her!

The labyrinth never ends. It jolts and shudders all around us, and I feel myself forgetting how I came here, where I'm running to, who I am.

I live it in dreams, over and over again. But despite my greatest efforts to change the vision, to somehow alter the desperate outcome, nothing changes. We never find our mother, before the end.

* * *

The sky is pale when I see it again, settling behind soft feather clouds and searching for contrast in the whiteness there. Morning. I breathe. It was just a dream. My lungs are stiff. How long have I lain here?

I find my elbows and sit up, noticing the give of a thick blanket spread under me, and the soft crinkling of grass beneath it. There's a girl, crouching several paces away, staring. Her fur is brighter than any I've seen before. Almost white.

"*Vyeht!* The dead wakes!" she gasps, and her green eyes gape wide at me like great shining stones in a snowy bed. I only blink in response, wondering for a moment whether I can recall how to speak. A boy appears before I can gather my words. He's a somewhat darker color—sand and earth shades streaked and mingled together. He kneels and shuffles slowly to the end of my blanket, extending a battered wooden bowl for me to hold. Water. It tastes like leather. Who are these two? Other survivors? I wonder for a moment, blinking blankly at their faces before I begin to notice an odd sensation in my lungs. Something . . . different. I pause with the bowl at my chin. . . . What's this feeling in my chest? It's warm and electric, kindled like a little flame just beneath my heart. It's churning, buzzing. *Empowering.*

I breathe deep, feel the sensation ripple through my knees, my back, my fingertips. It's a familiar kind of rushing. Something I've heard before—in the wind, in the river. In my dreams.

Energy.

My hands begin to tremble, and the water draws little circles in the bowl before me. I can hardly set it down before I'm rising to my feet. When did my bones become so light? I leap from the blanket and dart out across the thin grass, loose tunic flying like a cape at my back.

It's like a dream! Wind at my ears, earth at my feet! Coil, push, impact—the art of running rings out like an old, wonderful melody in my body. My legs already know the angles, the tension, the release. Heaving lungs! Racing heart!

I don't hear the others calling after me until I'm nearly three hilltops away, dancing and leaping in circles with my hands to the sky. Their voices echo worriedly after me, telling me to wait, but I don't care. Not now. I can't suppress the elated laugh that wells up in my throat. It pushes out tears as it comes, painting wet stripes down my cheeks.

Energy!

Something has happened. Some wild miracle, some unbelievable fortune. *I can run.* And I feel like I could run for days—from the eastern hills to the western mountains, if I chose. I keep circling through the grass, listening to the rhythm of the body—the blood, the breath. All the days of my strange life begin to come together in my mind, playing like an odd and hazy nightmare. Somehow, death has lost its grip. And for the first time in my waking memory, I feel *alive*—thoroughly, truly alive.

The two others come into view several hilltops away, shuffling slowly. I turn to them, beaming.

"I'm not dying anymore! *K'alvyolt'n!* It's a miracle!" I shout. My voice is almost shrill with excitement. I start toward them, watching the baffled looks they give me. The boy stands just behind the green-eyed girl, holding his shoulders in a loose and weary way that sparks something old in my memory. Loose shoulders, like someone I know, or once knew. . . .

Thayl!

How had I forgotten? My celebration meets an untimely end. The terrifying scene in the Citadel floods suddenly back to my mind's eye, and I find myself rushing to meet the two strangers on the next slope.

"Please, did you see someone else where you found me? Was there a dark-furred boy?"

The two of them exchange glances, and the girl shakes her head.

"There was no one," she tells me.

No one? I turn and glance over the surrounding landscape. Slow-rising green hills, dark walls of trees. No ruins in sight.

"Where . . . where's the Citadel?" I'm not sure how to sound.

"Citadel?"

"Yes," I say, and heaviness begins to swell in my stomach. "When I fell, I came from the Citadel. It was there. I was staring at it just before . . ." My words are lost in their troubled faces, falling to silence. Then the girl speaks.

"There was no Citadel," she tells me. "We found you here, not far from our camp. You were here when night came."

What?

My heart climbs into my throat. How could this be? The columns. . . . I remember seeing the gleam of the white columns, the wall of the Citadel atop the hill—and the Creature. I remember it all. How did I come to this place? My thoughts erupt all at once and collide in my head, piling up and becoming useless behind my teeth. And then I have no idea what to say. It's as if I've wandered too far into one of my dreams and found myself waking on some alternate plane of the reality I once knew.

Is Thayl still . . . ?

The thought shakes me. I can't wait here.

"How much have you seen of the ruined city? H-have you seen it at all?" I ask them at last, eyes darting between each of theirs.

"We've only just begun to explore the northern edge," the boy answers softly, his hand floating up to rest atop his head. His thinking pose.

"Then we're north of the ruins?" A little wave of relief washes over me. I turn to orient myself with the rising sun, finding south to my right. I can't delay. I nod to the strangers and thank them hurriedly before darting off over the hills again, heading south. The grass becomes tall as I go. But I don't let it slow me down. I leap and sail through the thin blades with elbows held high, leaving an uneven, trampled path in my wake.

The chill and soft gleam of morning are only beginning to fade when I spot the ruins rising calmly above the hills to the southeast. The haze that once hung so thickly over the land has thinned and dissipated, sliding back and coiling over the tops of the surrounding woods. Even from this distance, the Citadel's remaining spire can be seen—thin and haunting, silent and unmoving. Like the marker of a grave. Of *many* graves. I slow my pace, watching the faded shades of the Old City. And in an odd moment of silence it occurs to me: this is my home. I've always dwelt in a grave. But I'm alive now—how can I enter the grave again? I shake my head. There's no other option.

I find an entrance at the northwest bulk of the Citadel. Still intact, it's only wide enough for one or two individuals to walk comfortably at a time. Maybe a servant passage. Long and narrow, splitting off at dark intersections. I enter and round a corner, then pause, waiting for the black scene to fade into view. When it does, I follow the light that paints a soft glow along the walls. A glow only slightly less subtle than the shape of the corridors ahead. I go straight for a time, then right, then sharply to the left, and right again—into a cramped room full of cluttered shelves and dust-coated buckets. The closet ends in a narrow door that hangs partly off its hinges. I push through, squinting and swatting at the clumps of dust that dislodge and snow down onto my head. The hall beyond is broad and dimly lit—but light enough to let me see the blue and violet patterns along the tiled floor. And just beyond it—

The Domed Hall is dimmer than I remember. But it's only morning now. I stand at the top of the wide staircase and stare out across the open space, to the arched entryway in the opposite wall. The place where Thayl and I entered before. That time, we turned left.

"Thayl!" I call out to my right, and my voice echoes throughout the marble halls with an almost startling volume. Leaping down every corridor, rippling along the curves and bends of every open space in this massive, heaping dungeon. It continues until the sound is nothing more than a pure, ringing tone, then fades and dies softly in the cool shadows all around. I catch my breath, feeling stiff. Someone must have heard. Or some*thing*. But there's no reply. And suddenly I'm feeling strange. Uneasy. Just like before. I battle to suppress the thoughts that begin to rise in my mind, with little success. Maybe it was foolish to come here. Maybe it's too late. . . .

I make my way down the steps, then move along the outer curve of the circular floor below to the foot of the staircase at my right. Then begin to crawl soundlessly up on my hands and feet—leaning close to the cool stone. Only my head clears the top step, when I reach it. Just enough to gaze down the broad corridor lined with doorways. And I can see that the tremendous double doors at the far end of the passage have been opened—pushed as wide as their thick, corroding hinges permit to reveal the space beyond. The windowed corridor, the columned place with the shattered wooden desk—I see it all. For an instant. But then the thing in the doorway steals my attention. It's hazy at first, like an image wavering in the summer heat. But it isn't moving. It stands between the double doors with perfect stillness. I blink and look again, wondering if my perception has fooled me. But I know it hasn't. I feel the presence before I can think to question further. My skin begins to prickle all over as the fur stands subtly on end. My eyes begin to water impulsively. What *is* it?

Just back away. Back down the steps. Just get out of sight.

If only my limbs were as fast as my thoughts. I remain in place for an agonizing moment longer, crouched with my hands clawing the marble step before me. Then the figure in the doorway seems to shift, and what was blurred becomes suddenly vivid to my straining eyes. It's a man. A *man*. But what does that mean? What is a man?

My arms and legs come to life at last, and I push away from the steps before another breath can escape my lips. And I'm gone—running with my heart at my temples and all my bones aflame. I fly under the archway and down the passage where Thayl and I once entered, dashing over the tiles on the tips of my toes. I throw myself into the sunlight that pours from the place where we once climbed in, and come crashing down into the hot dirt beside the start of the Avenue. The landing sets me rolling, but I find my feet without delay and continue running, heading south again. And I don't stop until I find the others.

10

They come from each of the Ten Regions of the land, selected by the will of the people to stand as speakers of the Voice. They come to the high towers of Tekéhldeth like princes in shining robes and sashes—like heroes of uncharted potential. They come to the House of Voices with all the promises of their people held in tight fists, with lofty ambitions carefully arranged like constellations in their palms. Such plans, such hopes, they carry with them! They speak for their people. They are the First Officers of the Voice, the *Ts'ufi Afre*. They come as junior representatives. But few wish to remain as such.

The newest young officer, representative of the city people of Tekéhldeth itself, is no exception. Távihn Dredékoldn, acting Eviskyóneh of the eighty-first Era, could see it from the moment he first glimpsed the young noble entering at the grand southern steps of the House. There's a kind of burning in the eyes of the ambitious that Dredékoldn has learned to recognize throughout his long years in the House. The wish for power is a hot hunger, and it scalds the countenances of all who bear it. As the High Eviskyóneh, the Directing Hand, Dredékoldn holds final authority over all the House. But he never thirsted for it. The high office is only the burden he has been elected to bear. And he has borne it for eight years.

"Sekýnteo. Kyvóike Sekýnteo." The new officer's name is a strange sensation in Dredékoldn's throat. It's heavy, the way the name of a graveyard is heavy. Or the title of a war. And it's an old name, kept from the days of kingdoms.

Sekýnteo enters silently at the sound of his name, head bowed. It's a custom for the Eviskyóneh to personally welcome the new officers. Dredékoldn signals for the escorts to return to their posts, then extends a broad hand toward the chair across from his small desk. The young man settles into the seat with a soft sliding of silk, elbows loose and regal on the armrests. His smile is well practiced. Dredékoldn finds his own seat and folds his arms over the desk where the wood is worn smooth from the gesture.

"Young Sekýnteo," he begins, "you have been selected by the people of Tekéhldeth to be their Voice and Speaker within the walls of this House. Are you prepared to stand as a representative of their will?"

"Yes, High Eviskyóneh, sir. The burden is mine to bear." The new officer's voice carries the bell-tone of a singer.

"Then as Directing Hand I welcome you into the order of the Ts'ufi Afre, and this the House of Voices."

"I thank you, High Eviskyóneh." And he bows his head once more.

Then Dredékoldn holds out his arms, directing attention to the towering shelves that line the walls of his library.

"Do you know this room? This is the place of keeping for the records of all the Eviskyóneh," he explains, level voiced. "Even as a First Officer of the Voice, you may in time leave your print in the records of this place."

Sekýnteo turns to capture the many scrolls in his gaze before returning his attention to the older man across the desk.

"Yes, I intend to, high sir," he says. And something wild flutters behind the golden-brown of his eyes. The light plays a kind of dance in the flecks of color there, and Dredékoldn finds himself momentarily captured in the specter. The young officer's eyes are not unlike the stone of a pendant Dredékoldn once purchased from merchants on the far eastern shore and brought home for his lady, many years ago. A stone the color of dawn.

Who *is* this young Sekýnteo?

After a time of silence, the Eviskyóneh finds his voice and allows a soft "Indeed" to escape his throat. Then he blinks and stands, crossing an arm over his broad chest in the ceremonial fashion.

"Kyvóike Sekýnteo of the Ts'ufi Afre Division, may the Voice of the people ever support you."

The new officer rises, offering a gracious bow before mirroring the salute.

"May our service stem the cries of the Voice," he murmurs, completing the line. And then he turns away, letting a soft glance fall to the doors of the balcony beyond the seat of the Eviskyóneh before gliding from the room in silence. And then he is gone.

Dredékoldn finds himself sighing in relief. He carries an odd presence with him, that Sekýnteo. And why had he looked—

"Father, I don't like him. I don't like him at all."

The boy appears at the entry to the balcony, half hidden behind the painted doors. Even at eight years old, he holds himself with the kind of cool resolve so common to the adult residents of the House. And he has his mother's dark hair.

"No doubt there's something odd about the new officer," Dredékoldn replies, not entirely surprised to find the boy listening from the balcony. Some men would chastise their sons for such eavesdropping. But this time, Dredékoldn is only glad to have a witness. "But he may yet make a strong leader."

The boy turns to gaze out over the city beyond the stone railing, unconvinced. Far to the west, the sun is finding its resting place, sending its orange and yellow tendrils to drape across the walls and jagged rooftops of Tekéhldeth, the City of Glimmering Lights. The Golden City. It will be a calm night.

11

It turns out even a truly living body grows weary, eventually. But even as I let myself flop onto the grass near the base of the hill, I feel my strength returning. I've found the two strangers almost exactly where I left them. Their little camp wasn't difficult to locate—just a short run beyond the northern edge of the ruins. I merely retraced my own path in the tall hill-grass.

I didn't find him.

The six survivors we left behind were still camped at the place where we saw them last. They were hunting mice and rats among the ruins of a collapsed house when I discovered them, just east of the shelter where Kehlvi died. They'd learned to move their collected energy, pulling the strength from many limbs and combining it into one pair of legs. The result was an impressive burst of speed for the chosen hunter. And the thought of fresh meat had set them into an excited frenzy when I found them. But they only fell silent and shook their heads when I mentioned Thayl.

I ran everywhere. I searched the orchard, the river, and each of our hiding places in between. Calling his name when I dared. Then, heading north again, I passed along the western edge of the Citadel, glancing up at the columns as I panted along. I even followed along the wide curve of the outer wall until the place where I fell came into view. And I called out one last time. But there was no one. Even the massive body of the Creature had vanished.

"How do you do it?" The sandy-colored boy tips forward onto his knees when I sit to rest at last. He's almost trembling. "How do you overcome the weariness?" He speaks of it the way one might mention a fatal disease, with hushed and wavering words—as if speaking of the plague could somehow make our reality worse. Maybe that's what it is. A disease. Or *was*. How can I find the right words?

"By sensing and moving energy," I tell him. It's the best description I can manage. "It began when . . . I just . . . remembered something. When I was listening to the wind, and the river. It was like *hak'eunde,* a recollection—the body remembering the way it's supposed to work, or the way it once worked, when the weariness never happened."

I think back to that day in the rushing water, to the moment when I clapped my hands onto a shining fish and pulled the fire from its writhing muscle. It started with small energy, with stealing. We learned to feel the strength at our fingertips and tear it out like a rag from tight fists. It started with *taking.* But something's changed.

That final moment in the Citadel has remained a vivid, flashing scene in my mind. The sensation of Thayl's thin hands at my back—and the searing burst of electricity that rippled out from that point to fill my entire frame. Somehow, he reversed the original motion, turned back the wave. He didn't take; he *gave.* Gave so much that it raged along my spine and flooded into the broken places, waking something strange and ancient within me. Somehow, I'm healed. I can feel the way it moves—the way the energy courses along its path, weaving through my living body, generated within itself. I will never lack it again. But how was it unlocked?

I look back into the boy's expectant eyes.

"I'll teach you what I know," I tell him, glancing to his green-eyed sister, who watches from nearby. "Maybe in time we can solve it together."

Ilith and Ekyán. Siblings. They're the first new survivors I've seen since the time we found Kehlvi and Saiven, and they learn almost as quickly as Thayl. We spend all the afternoon sitting in the low shadow of the hill, arranged in a little circle with arms linked and breaths even, concentrating. I teach them to listen, to feel—to trace the hot flow of energy in the body. It's a wonderful thing, to see the way their eyes catch aflame with the first crawling sensations, the way hope and relief pour slowly over their weary faces and open their lungs to the wind. They're sharing strength before sunset.

* * *

I dream of Évrieth again, when night comes. I find her standing near the columns of a wide and shining hall, smiling at the morning light that streams in and paints the white stone all around her. The whiteness is blinding.

"We can live forever now, can't we?" I ask her, and my voice rings and hiccups out into the brightness, echoing forever. Her smile only broadens. I raise a hand to my eyes, squinting at the open air.

"Évrieth," I begin again, "do you remember Man?" She turns then, ivory dress swaying softly at her ankles.

"Have you forgotten already?" she questions in reply. There's a kind of playfulness in her voice that I can't understand. Somewhere in the white abyss, a subtle wind passes by, waking the gentle, resonating voice of unseen chimes.

"What is Man?" I ask her. "Will you tell me?" Even as the question passes out of me, I can feel it pulling like a weight at my chest. I knew the answer once, didn't I?

Évrieth doesn't answer me. She only crosses the space between us and takes my hand. And her grasp is warm.

12

When morning returns we eat food unlike any I've tasted—pressed fruit; dried meats; and dense, crisped breads. It's a strange feeling to find plentiful food in my stomach. A comfort, but somehow no longer such a tremendous necessity. And when the evening falls, Ilith and Ekyán show me where they found it.

We take an odd path through the trees, turning here and there, weaving and circling through the foliage, ducking our heads. They say it puts off followers. Not long ago, the concept would have confused me. But now I wonder how I managed to wander through the ruins of the Old City for so long without noticing that crawling sensation at my back—that pulsing urge to glance over my shoulder with every wary step.

We turn northward for a time, then south again, drifting westward all the while. In time we come to a wooded gorge, where a little stream has carved deep into the wet earth and the stones jut out from the moss at sharp and sudden angles. Our path leads through the gorge, over the steep bank at the far side and into a more ancient wood, where the massive bodies of the trees rise like great dark pillars all around, blanketing the soil with their red needles.

I begin to spot a peculiar shape through the leaves. It rises like a boulder among the evening shadows, boasting a pale, sandy color that paints oddly against the dark hues of the trees. But it can't be stone— it's too perfectly shaped, too soft at the edges, too pale in the failing light. And there's more than one. The others come slowly into view as we duck from one tree to the next. Then I can see more clearly. They're shelters.

Circular and slant-roofed, staked to the forest floor by massive spikes of dark metal.

A world of smells washes over us as we creep silently toward the camp—sticky smoke and animal skins, singed bark and old leaves. And there's one other scent in the night air, thick and bitter—a scent I've smelled once before. I take another breath, let the smell find a winding path through my recollections. And then my heart flutters. The Creature. It's the smell of the Creature. I glance toward the others, wondering if they know, if they've seen it. But they remain calm. Ilith leads the way now, maneuvering in the shadows to catch a clear view of each shelter's thickly-flapped and fastened openings, searching for motion. She's done it before. There's only stillness in the camp. The doors of the shelters all appear to open toward the great, black pit at the center of the clearing—where the remnants of a massive fire lie, still smoldering in dark piles. I can't seem to turn away from the doors as we pass them by.

Doors. A seal to keep the world out. Or to hide behind, out of sight. I can only begin to guess what hides behind them.

Ilith waves her pale arm beside me, hastening me along. I swallow and do my best to follow in silence. Just beyond the western-most tent we find the boxes— stacked and covered like square drums, sealed with thin leather stretched tightly across their tops. We move quickly, breathlessly. Ekyán swiftly shows me how to release the latches at the sides of the boxes. Inside there are all kinds of wonderful-smelling foods. Fruits, breads, meats—all neatly wrapped and organized in their places. We take enough for several days, laying it carefully in the blanket satchel tied over my shoulders. The fruit presses awkwardly against my back, but it isn't heavy. I nod to the others, and Ilith motions soundlessly to the northern trees. We begin to slip away.

Out of sight.

A kind of urgency begins like soft thrumming in my lungs as we creep away, rising steadily. I send another glance over the camp—to the tall shelters with their silent doors, the smoldering ashes of the fire's bed. No monster in sight. We move along another winding path for our return trip—bending low as we go, sharing energy at intervals without slowing our step. The others need it for speed. If only they could run.

The camp is quickly veiled behind the trees at our backs as we turn eastward, and the blackness of the night begins to close gently in all around us, folding like a dark cloak at our shoulders. I let out my breath. We're alive; we're headed back.

But we aren't alone. Somehow, I suddenly know it. We're almost to the edge of the gorge when I spot our company—crouched like a dark, massive bird in the lowest arms of a nearby tree. It's hunched over, one thick arm reaching for support to a branch over its head. Watching us. It's one of them. My hand flies up and claps onto Ilith's shoulder. She turns, green eyes wet and shining. But my voice is tangled in my throat. I turn abruptly southward, pressing her to follow, tugging Ekyán with my other hand.

Out of sight!

They follow the motion without asking, and we shuffle along the ragged edge of the gorge until I lose count of the trees. My steps are awkward in the darkness, and the sound is maddening—thumping and crunching that seem to thunder out in all directions, despite my best attempt at silence. *Anything* could follow us. But as far as I'm able to sense, nothing does. We find a boulder-flooded path into the gorge and begin our descent, breath caught like little pebbles in our throats. And I only look back once.

We'll sleep in shifts tonight.

13

The word rises like the evening smoke, spreads and settles like fog in the streets. It catches the morning wind, puffing and whirling like little cyclones in the alleyways.

Sekýnteo. Sekýnteo the Wise, Sekýnteo the Noble. The man of justice, man of miracles. The man who rose like no other through the ranks of the House. In only six years he climbs to the high seats of the Honored, where the old men marvel at his natural authority and reason and grace.

Sekýnteo of the Voice. His name becomes a shout of good fortune in the streets of Tekéhldeth, a label lifted high on floating banners for all the lands to see. Sekýnteo the Bright, Sekýnteo the Golden. The man who captures hopes and lifts them high above the shining towers of the city.

14

I notice the leaves dancing at my chin and make an effort to slow my breath, willing it to nothing more than a whisper at my nose. The leaves here catch the light and throw it at odd angles, brightening the scene with a speckled mix of brilliant greens and grays and yellows. I glance stiffly through the trees to my right and spot Ekyán poised and solid in his place, crouching with his head almost leveled to his knees. The sun falls in blotches over his streaked fur, merging with the colors there. It's remarkable how well he blends into the leaves.

We're learning silence. It's taken most of the morning to reach this point. We came here together. Ekyán turns to catch my gaze, then nods in silent confirmation. I prepare to move, checking my balance and shrugging away the dull ache in my shoulders. I need to be fast. It isn't the first boar we've managed to surprise.

The poor beast lets out a sharp and sudden squeal when Ekyán leaps out from the shade of the trees. It startles me almost to stillness—I shake the cold ringing from my ears as I tear through the leaves. The boar darts like a fleeing shadow between the trees, crazed and terrified. Dry earth flies up and showers down in its wake as it darts on a northeastward path. A fast creature. But an unfortunate one, all the same. I meet it only several paces from my hiding place and throw my weight into my leap. I catch the boar with an arm across its heaving breast, and we crash awkwardly against the forest floor. Sky, leaves, branches, dirt— they toss and jab and prickle all around us. The strength flows like hot water from the boar's writhing muscle, and its wild heart falls still and silent before our tumbling ends at the base of a massive tree.

I'm still struggling to roll the limp beast off my leg when Ilith comes sliding into view with her hands resting on her narrow hips. Her white fur is almost overwhelming, reflecting the midday sun like the pale and ruined towers of the Old City. I frown, squinting up at her.

"I like to think that someday it'll be my turn," she tells me, eyeing the kill at her feet. I manage to free my leg and ease into a low squat beside the boar.

"Me too," I breathe, swatting the dirt from my knees. My fingers flex impulsively at my sides, buzzing with the flow of new energy. I hadn't meant to take it all. The others could've used the boost. "It'd be wonderful if more of us could run."

We've spent the last eight nights with the other six survivors who were with us the night Kehlvi died, in another hidden shelter not far from the orchard. And in the past several weeks we've managed to catch almost every kind of leaping, crawling, trotting creature in the southwestern woods. Hunting has become our survival. *Hitérian*, "shifting," makes it possible—the skill of energy shifting that's become such a critical ability among us. Hitérian. It soothes the awful weariness in our bones, ebbs the tide of hunger at our throats, slows the advance of that strange and silent death that we once so hopelessly accepted. Hitérian is our chance at hope. Hope unlike any we've ever thought possible. But we aren't complete. Not yet.

We drag our kill to the eastern edge of the trees, where the leaves and shade fall away and the hills begin. I'm grateful for the tarp. Ekyán pulled it from a broken awning near the Avenue only two weeks ago, and we've used it to wrap and drag away all but the smallest catches ever since. The load is less when we pull together. We're shoulder to shoulder, bent like young trees in the wind as we move over the grass. The ruins rise just beyond the hills ahead—a dark and jagged wave, silent but not sleeping along the horizon. Fortunately, the sun is high but gentle, laying its rays like warm breath at our backs. We'll need more than a few rests before it sinks again. We found the boar in a grove of trees not far from the banks of the river. Now the return journey will likely consume the entire afternoon.

Our path cuts a long angle through the southwestern edge of the ruins, through a place where the broken houses stand divided between low, crumbling walls and long-forsaken gardens. I stare into the little plots as we pass them by, trying to imagine how they must have once looked—before they were shattered and torn and entangled in the wild arms of climbing vines. Before the rain and wind had done their work. These were homes, once. For *someone*.

We're near the edge of the city when we take our first rest. Ilith trudges to the grass beyond the fallen stones the moment our load is dropped and flings herself down—limbs spread out from her body on all sides.

"*T'ehvt'an!* Sweet rest!" she gasps, and her little voice is caught like a feather in the wind—whisked up and away over the afternoon hills. Ekyán only smiles and stretches his thin arms, too tough to accept the luxury of the grass. They make me glad, these two.

I step in an idle circle beside the wrapped boar, already re-energized, then look northward along the little cobble path that leads away into the city's outer, narrow lanes. It's a simple place, a peaceful place. And it's something else. I stare again, wondering at the tingling at the edge of my thought.

It's something else, isn't it?

I begin to wander lazily along the battered cobble, bending slightly here and there to see beyond the sharp turns ahead. It's a different sort of feeling, residing here—like a forgotten name or errand, floating just beyond my reach. Something speaks here—something about the way the wind plays over the stones, about the way the sun falls and bleaches the pavement—that turns little eddies in my mind. Then I've stopped without realizing it, standing where the path splits and sends an arm toward the west. For a moment, I can't think at all. My thoughts freeze in their places and fall like little crystals from my mind, and I forget them. For a moment, I know only the place before me, the broken house at the corner of the fork in the lane.

The blurred memory comes so suddenly—like a gust of wind billowing over me, like waking with a start in the night. This house. This place. . . .

Lorëu!

My sister's desperate voice rings back like an old echo in my mind. This is the place. The place where memories began, the place my dreams are endlessly chasing. This is the place where I once belonged—a place of love and laughter, of long talks and warm firelight, of old songs and white-clouded summers. Where Évrieth found my name and pulled me like an empty bottle from the grave. This is the place where an older life once existed. And where my waking life began.

Until they begin to spot and splatter along my neck, I don't notice the tears. But now I can't stop them.

Home! Mother! Father!

They must have existed once, long ago—yet only yesterday. Somehow they're lost to me, buried in this strange and startling world I know, this mystery of living and dying, waking and dreaming, forgetting and remembering. How can I ever find them again?

. . . and Thayl?

I become suddenly more aware of the aching in my knees and shoulders, and let myself sink to the dry ground. It's an aching that's grown for days. Now it seems to magnify the weight in my chest, pressing in on my lungs.

Where have they all gone? Where are they now?

A soft hand appears at my shoulder, and I turn to find Ekyán's simple, silent face beside me. Somehow, he doesn't need to ask.

"Ekyán," I whisper, "do you know who you are? Do you remember what we are?"

The boy only pulls his lip into a gentle frown and stares back at me for a time, then turns away with flat ears angled back, shaking his head. Maybe we'll find out together. Someday.

15

It's a warm night, when the son of Dredékoldn wakes in the stillness of his bedchamber. The sort of night that wraps and cradles in all around, spinning vivid dreams into sleepers' minds with its warmth and mist and silence. But there's something bitter in the air, this night. And the boy is restless.

It's a black summer night, only five days beyond his fourteenth birthday. He pulls a loose tunic from the chair at his bedside and slips it over his shoulders, almost shivering as the cool silk slides over his spine. The great marble halls of the House are often empty, yet rarely silent. The arched corridors capture all the voices of the city and send them echoing out along the walls, bouncing here then there and back again. The shouts of voices in the distant streets, the morning cries of birds and running children. And when evening comes, the thin and lonesome ringing of the nightflies. But this night there's a different sound.

It happens so strangely, when the son of the Eviskyóneh enters in through the great red doors of the West Corridor in the deepest hour of the night. It plays out like the terrible scenes of children's nightmares. But the boy isn't sleeping.

He isn't sleeping when he pauses just beyond the entrance to his father's study with a sudden, hot wetness at his feet. He isn't sleeping when he sees the dark and spreading puddle along the patterned carpet before him, or when he turns to find his father lying in the midst of it—struggling, life hanging in a final gasp at his bloodied lips. The boy isn't sleeping, but awake— suddenly more awake and aware than any child should ever need to be. Awake enough to see every cruel and crooked line in the face of the man who stands beyond the dying Eviskyóneh, in whose hand the freshly blackened blade hangs loose and casual. The man whose face the boy could never mistake—not since the day he first saw him enter at the great steps of the House, only six years before. The man who is adored and beloved of all the people of Tekéhldeth. The man who comes rushing now, spearing at the son with the blade that slew the father, laughing hoarsely at the boy who slips and nearly stumbles backward into the tiled hall as he flees, leaving bloody footprints in his path.

It's a warm night, when the son of the eighty-first Eviskyóneh runs until his father's blood is dried on his feet. He runs with the terror of a hunted animal, calling and pounding at the doors he passes, never daring to pause for long. But there's no one to hear. His voice rings out in vain through the grand halls of the House. Even the servants' quarters are dark and lifeless. And that's where he finds the others—men with knives and studded rods and stone faces.

He's only fourteen when he flees from the House of Voices and into the narrow streets of Tekéhldeth, tear-streaked and bloodstained and breathless. The night that would remain forever burned into the folds of his young memory, beside the grimacing face of Kyvóike Sekýnteo.

16

"You don't need to come."

She secures her sash as she speaks, crossing the fold over her shoulder and around her waist, then finishing the knot at her back. "Five of us can go together. We'll make a chain. The runner would be plenty fast." I can hear the forced edge on her voice. The subtle attempt to convince herself.

"Five would probably be too noisy," I tell her, sitting up. "And what if the runner slips up? It wouldn't be easy to make another chain once you're drained." My knees are less firm than I had hoped, but the shelter's slanting wall makes a decent brace. Mornings are hardest. Ilith watches, shaking her head.

"You're like a stiff log," she whines.

"I'm feeling fine," I breathe back at her. I move along the wall and into the light, where the plaster gapes open and lets the early sun slide in, watching my feet all the while. She's standing close when I look up—paused with her glossy, meadow-green eyes near enough for me to watch the light darting like gentle sparks in the shadows there.

"This time," she says, calm and stern. "Then that's it, until your pains ease. You'll kill yourself without rest."

I nod. She's like Évrieth, but with sharper edges. Always insisting that we take better care of ourselves, speaking sternly with her chin tipped and her back straightened, never satisfied. But she does it all with a funny smirk at her mouth and a kind of singing in her eyes. And the warmth that radiates there is almost tangible. I sometimes wonder if she'll live to be a mother someday. She'd make a good one.

The pains have gotten worse. What began as subtle soreness in my knees and shoulders has grown into constant throbbing, and the panging in my chest has swelled and spread into my sides and back. Even sitting up has become a chore. This morning my elbows have stiffened. I sit outside in the morning light while the others prepare, turning my arms in slow circles, willing them to bend past the pain.

Ilith thinks it's overexertion, from the constant demands of hunting and energy exchange. I'm almost always the chosen runner when we hunt together. But it makes sense. Despite all our efforts, despite countless nights of concentrated hitérian and enthusiastic ideas, we have yet to replicate my unique case. We have yet to reverse the order, to *give* rather than take. For a month now I've lived among the others as the only survivor who can move quickly without fainting, who can remain on my feet without tiring. I'm the only one who can *run*—and keep running, if the kill slips from my grasp. And we hunt nearly every day. Overexertion, she says. Maybe she's right. But the pains are odd, disconnected and spread throughout my body. And they grow worse when I lie still.

Now and then, I wonder if I've only fooled myself. Perhaps I never really escaped the plague of our people. Perhaps Thayl's gift of energy was only the slowing of an inevitable tide—a tide that's already begun to sweep and swell all around me, irreversible. Perhaps these are the pains of a failing body. But I try not to think of it.

We're heading deep into the western forests today, beyond the river and toward the mountains, further than we've ever dared to venture. It's a journey the three of us have intended to make for some time. Our first attempt to venture so far outside the borders of our land in search of new territory. In search of *anything* more than the rubble and ruin we've known—anything to confirm the idea that other civilizations and cities may still stand, somewhere. That the world still exists, beyond the hills and trees that form our cradle.

We don't take much. The way is long—too long to carry more than a little satchel of water and a handful of food in the folds of our sashes. We'll find all we need along the way. I wrap my own sash before we leave, crossing it over my shoulder and weaving the folds around my waist. It ends in a knot at my back, dyed dark, like the color of the evening sky. Unfolded, it's wide enough to be a blanket. Most of our sashes have come from the collapsed shops along the western side of the ruins. We've found all sorts of uses for them—from carrying food and tools to keeping us warm at night. But aside from their practical uses, the sashes simply *feel* right. We wrap and tie them in ways that our hands remember, unable to explain the meaning to ourselves. And we begin to wear them with a kind of silent confidence—as if determined to revive an old tradition, despite the utter lack of history in our minds.

I found mine in the remains of my own home, lying unsoiled, partly folded in the space beneath a fallen door. It belonged to my family. Somehow, I'm certain of it. My only true possession.

We come to the river before the morning has lost its chill, to a spot where the water grows thin and rapid for a time, tumbling angrily over the dark boulders that rest in its way. Here and there the stones rise like black and broken mountain peaks from the waves, clothed in part by the invasion of moss, with sides worn smooth against the watery surge. They're our bridge. We cross with delicate motions, clutching the moss as we go—careful not to slip into the water's cold and merciless grasp. I'm not sure how well any of us could swim in the rapids. And none of us want to find out.

A new forest lies beyond. A land we've never seen. The land beyond the river. We pause only long enough to satisfy our thirst at the rocky riverbank, then continue westward through the woods until the sun hangs its orange gleam low in the western canopy of the trees. Walking all the while with nothing but the birds and fretful rodents to accompany us.

"Do you hear it?" Ekyán is always the first to hear anything. We've paused to share energy when he speaks with his ears tipped back and his nose in the air. The trees are young and pale skinned here, and the lowering sun pulls a pleasant color from their bodies, spreading a warm glow throughout the branches. So yellow! I hold my breath and follow Ekyán's gaze to the northwest, listening. It *is* there—faint and restless, like the voice of the river from afar. But different.

"Does the river split and branch this way?" Ilith appears between us, water satchel in hand. No one knows. I glance back toward the east before turning westward again. The shadows are stretching.

"The light's failing," I remind them. "Where should we settle for the night?" Ekyán can't seem to pull his gaze from the distance, from the sound that plays endlessly at the edges of the trees.

"Let's just have a look," he whispers, and he begins to shuffle ahead. "We can find a place there."

The source of the sound isn't far. We feel toward it, creeping nearer until the air grows damp and the rushing voice swells to a tumbling roar. It's something I've never seen—or even imagined, when we find it. A dark cliffside rises sharply among the trees ahead, cold and jagged, looming like an ancient city wall above the trees. A curtain of water pours from the tall brow of the stone, somewhere high and out of sight, and comes cascading down in a wild flurry against the rocks below. It swirls and leaps where it lands, pooling first, then funneling into a narrow stream that curves away southward into the woods. For a moment we're motionless, standing dumbly with mouths hanging open, unsure how to admire the view. Even from many paces away, we can feel the soft rain on our faces. A cool, flickering mist, weighty with the scent of leaves and stones and wet earth.

Waterfall.

The word comes from some unnamed place in my memory, but I don't question it. And I don't want to. It's a magical thing. Ilith is the first to find her voice again. And a soft "Oh yes" is all she can manage. As if some part of her had expected the scene. Maybe she came here before, long ago.

We could admire the watery spectacle for hours. But nightfall presses us onward. We find a low shelf in the rocks to the east of the falls, where the mist fades but the sound of the water is only gently dulled. The rhythm is calming. And it feels good to have something firm at our backs. Safe. We fit nicely there together, slouched between the folds of the cliff face.

I volunteer for the first watch. Sleep will only stiffen my already aching body. Staying awake somehow keeps my joints loose and dulls the swelling discomfort in my lungs. I set my back to a corner and stretch out my legs in a mild attempt to feel comfortable. Ilith and Ekyán are asleep before I can loosen my sash.

* * *

I'm awake but not watching when they come. It may've been foolish—resting in the stone where the roar of the falls hides away all the subtle sounds of the night. Where the rustling of leaves and the wary shifting of animals in the shadows can't be heard. They come when my thoughts have taken me somewhere far away, when the soft fluttering of the day's memories has lulled me almost to sleep. When I see them at last, it's too late. Somehow, they've found us.

They reach for Ekyán first. He's near the edge, easiest to snatch. And then we're all awake, scrambling for purchase on the rocks. Thick arms, violent hands—they find and jerk Ekyán from the ledge and onto the forest floor, then snap away when he pulls the strength from their grip. But others come, grabbing and surrounding him from every angle. And they begin to shout, bellowing to one another with their deep and terrible voices, shaking the soil with their stomping.

There's no time, no time!

For an instant, I'm helpless with shock, useless to change the scene that's unfolding in front of me. But something shifts in my blood as I watch, and I find myself suddenly leaping into motion. Terror throws me beyond the line of hesitation, beyond the place where doubts are born and contemplated. It awakens an ancient place in my bones. A place where we must *survive.*

Ekyán!

I fling myself onto the back of the nearest Creature and tear the hot energy from its massive, coiling muscles. It lets out a wail, arching its spine before slumping to the earth beneath me. Somewhere to my left, Ilith takes down another. I dart through the legs of the next and cling to the beast that holds Ekyán by his tunic. Its hulking knees buckle like great, sodden logs when I steal the life from them. And then, for an instant, we're all free. We turn to rush southward through the black woods, hands linked, using hitérian to boost our speed. If only we could keep running, if only—

An abrupt, backward tug across my chest jerks the breath from my throat, and I'm still gasping when a rope coils mercilessly around my thin arms. I fight with all my might. Kick and claw, bite and thrash. One attacker falls back with a startled scowl when I use my foot to pull the energy from its grip. But others come. Soon enough the night vanishes entirely and I'm scooped into the folds of a massive sack, thrown over-shoulder like a fresh kill. Helpless.

Breathe, breathe. There must be a way.

I strain at the rope that binds my arms, hoping desperately to pull energy from the back of the Creature that bears me. But something interrupts my touch. Something thick and dense, something that clatters softly as my weight bumps repeatedly into it. Like wooden armor.

Armor.

In a moment of stillness I'm struck by the plainness of it all. They were prepared. They *knew*. There's no way to escape. The reality collides like a sudden stone against my heart. And I wonder how far Ilith and Ekyán will flee before they catch them.

17

They stand atop a high tower when they speak to the people. Shouting, declaring. Raising their hard fists to the sky. They send their voices like wild sirens over the city, send them quaking along the rooftops, the shutters, the dusty brick walls—catching the hearts of the people and setting them aflame. Their voices spike like static in the streets, calling for outrage, calling for vengeance. They strike their chests and call for judgment against the wicked murderer of the High Eviskyóneh. The slayer whose guilt was confirmed by his bloody prints at the scene. The traitorous child who dared to tear the life from his own father's breast.

It was the brave Sekýnteo who found the Eviskyóneh where he fell, who held the poor man as he gasped his last breaths, they say. It was the righteous Sekýnteo who sent the House guards in pursuit of the wretched killer. The murderer who managed to flee from the great halls of the House and into the night. But they will find him, they cry. They will find him.

The officers of the Voice swear with kingly indignation, when they speak to the people from a high tower in Tekéhldeth. Swear by the blood in their veins to avenge—until all the city is alive and leaping with the fire of their words. They will find him.

18

I'm alive . . . still alive. Alive, with the thick scent of the Creatures all around me, with the memory of Kehlvi's bloody death flashing across my mind. Maybe they'll do worse to me.

No!

There'll be another chance. A chance to fight, a chance to run. I can run. And fighting them off will only make me faster. I can run!

I'm in the bag for an eternity. And when it opens at last, tipping me into a rough and confining wooden cage, I'm almost blinded by the moonlight that beams into my face. It falls in a silver sheen from behind the Creatures' looming shoulders, obscuring their faces. There are so many of them. Tall, shadowed figures. The lid to my prison falls shut overhead with a stiff, wooden clap. Then they roll the entire frame lengthwise, and I struggle to raise my bound arms to shield my head against the tumbling. My shoulders throb terribly when it ends. And I can hardly hear beyond the wild thrumming of my heart at my temples. Their voices are deep and strange to me, garbling together and murmuring like the dull rustling of leaves or the jostling of rocks in the sand. Jostling all around me.

Will they try to eat me?

The cage smells like animals. I huddle at the center and try to watch them all at once, waiting, ready to dodge their attacks. I'm sure they'll try to jab at me, poke through the slats with their massive spears and cruel hands. But they don't. They don't move. They don't touch me at all. Their voices end, and they stand in a loose circle around the cage, staring quietly at their prize, nodding back and forth to one another. The new silence torments me. I hardly dare to breathe, to blink. My heart is almost bursting from its place when they turn away at last. And they leave. Slowly, reluctantly. They turn and disappear into the surrounding night, beyond the trees and into the camp at my back.

The camp. Until this moment I hadn't seen it there. The hulking canvas shelters, the smoking fire pit—almost identical to the one I saw with Ilith and Ekyán once before. They've taken me to their camp. I turn my head when they've gone and strain to watch for movement among the shelters. But I see nothing. I suppose even monsters need to sleep. Somehow, the thought helps my breath ease. At least I have until morning to ponder my fate. Or change it.

For a time, I'm too terrified to move. I look through my knees to the slats below, where the grass pokes up in random clumps. The wood is dark and weather stained, made ragged with deep grooves and scratches. The desperate marks of wild animals, no doubt. Is that what I am? Suddenly, I'm not sure anymore.

Whatever the Creatures are, they have brains. Brains enough to hunt us down with armor, to build tents and dirty animal cages. And they all wear clothes. Lots of it. I shake the images from my head and try to think of other things.

Ilith. Ekyán.

Maybe they escaped. Maybe they're hiding somewhere now, wondering what became of me, or if they'll ever see me again. I wonder if they'll make it back to the others. They'll be slow, with less hitérian to push them. I close my eyes.

Ilith! Ekyán!

My hands are choked in the rope. It traps my arms against my chest and ends in a cramped knot somewhere behind my head. I try to wiggle the tips of my tangled fingers, urge the blood into motion. The pains are returning along my limbs. But I do my best to think past them. I'm not dead yet. I have this night. A handful of desperate hours. The least I can do is try.

I look again at the slats beneath my feet. They rolled the cage to rest on its lid, after they dumped me inside. *Rolled.* I take a moment to shuffle onto my knees, hunched with my shoulders pressed into the upper corner of my prison. It doesn't take much to tip—it tips more suddenly than I had anticipated, and I tumble clumsily with the rolling motion.

Roll!

It isn't the greatest idea. But it's something. Something at least to give me a little hope until sunrise. Maybe I could roll back to the waterfall, to the river. I catch myself imagining impossible scenarios and bat them quickly from my mind. *Focus.*

Wedge, tip, tumble. I wonder if the sound carries far. Wedge, tip, and tumble again. Just to the edge of the trees, just out of sight, moving away from the camp one roll at a time. Hope starts to glimmer at the edge of my mind. Five rolls from the starting point. Five rolls from the nightmare, another toward morning. . . .

I'm leaning into the sixth when I spot my company. It's standing just beyond the nearest tent, motionless. Watching. I stiffen in my place, frozen with my shoulder to the corner of my cage. It must have heard the thumping. I see the turning of its shoulders as it glances slowly from side to side. And I can't stand the way my stomach twists at the sight of it. Those thick limbs—that long, terrible stature. It starts toward me, and I wonder for a moment if my heart will fail me.

Courage! If only my hands were free. . . .

The Creature needs only four long strides to close the space between us. And then it's crouching just beyond the dark wooden slats of my box, little eyes staring out from the blue wrap that swathes its head and face. My eyes can't open any wider, straining to hold back the tears. I can't suppress a terrified tremble when the visitor unfolds its arms and extends its pale, broad palms for me to see. Massive, empty hands.

"Don't be afraid."

For a moment, I'm almost certain I imagined it. The voice is low, resonating like slow-rolling thunder. I keep my spine pressed to the cage wall, fighting hopelessly to still the trembling in my knees.

"I won't hurt you."

This time I can't question. It *is* the Creature's voice. Undoubtedly male. They can speak our language? I stare back, tight jawed. His gaze is calm.

"What happened to you?" he whispers to me, and I notice an odd tilting in his voice, as if the words are new to his mouth. Assuming he has something like a mouth under those wraps. "Do you remember?"

I don't know how to respond.

"I've been watching your people for quite some time. The sharp air here in the lower lands doesn't seem to harm you, as it harms us. I told them not to go after you, told them how dangerous your people are," he murmurs, searching my stare. At long last my voice arrives at my throat, though weak and quivering.

"Dangerous. . . ." I swallow. "How . . . what?"

The Creature is unmoving. But the light in his eyes seems to shift when I speak.

"Dangerous, yes," he says. "You took down Faldálen."

"I . . ."

"In the ruins, a month ago." His voice is level. "Just you. And he was a big man. The others don't know. They don't understand your speech." His words clash and clamor in my ears, fighting for significance.

In the ruins . . . a month ago . . .

My mind rages, and suddenly the images come back to me—the Citadel, the Creature that attacked me. I shuffle uncomfortably in the rope, unable to pull my stare from the dark eyes that have captured me.

"There was no Citadel. . . . You were here when night came."

Ilith's words echo in my mind. It was him, that day. He was there. He moved the Creature's body. And he must have moved me. The thought sends another tremor through my aching lungs. And there was another word. A word he spoke that itches at my memory's edge.

"It was . . . you were there. But . . ." I'm fumbling pitifully for words, choking back the fear that still holds me stiffened in place. The Creature rests a thick hand on the wood before him.

"I had seen enough to know that you deserved to live. I knew the others would find you where I left you."

Somewhere nearby in the night, a handful of nightflies have begun their strange melody. A melody that's lulled me to sleep more times than I could hope to count. A song that's worked steadily into my dreams. I begin to find my breath again.

"What do you want from us?" I whisper.

For a moment he doesn't reply, doesn't move at all. And when he moves at last, reaching in through the cage wall and jerking the knot of rope up and over my head in one, fluid motion, I can scarcely think enough to gasp. The coil loosens along my arms, falling in a limp pile at my wrists. I shake the life back into my throbbing limbs and stare dumbfounded at the Creature squatting beyond the slats. I can't make sense of it, *any* of it—but part of me doesn't need to. Part of me is too exhilarated at the chance of survival to care. A tremendous part of me.

"I'll tell you what I *don't* want," he whispers, and he rises to his full, towering height. "I don't want to see you in this cage when morning comes."

Then he turns away, leaving his gaze until the very last moment—stalking back into the camp and vanishing behind the shadows there. Gone.

My hands are scrambling to find the lid, fingering madly at the latch that holds it—all long before my mind can pull away from the encounter I've just had. I stick my face to the wood and try to catch a decent glimpse of the mechanism. It's a metal device unlike any I've seen, but it's simple enough. There's no lock. I rattle the moving parts until the little door to my prison swings suddenly open. And then I'm running. Every muscle screaming in the effort, every tendon tight and wrenching in its place. I stumble blindly through the trees, unsure of any direction. The pains swell all over, rising sharply along my spine and shocking my lungs. Ahead, the world begins to tilt and sway. But I run on, curling my arms about my aching sides as I go.

Out of sight! Just get out of sight!

Shades of gray, sharp shadows, and blurring lines—the world begins to bleed together in my half-open eyes, and I struggle to understand it.

Overexertion.

I can't suppress a wet cough. At this rate, they could easily find and capture me again. If I could just fade into the roots of the trees, if I could slide beneath the shadows there. I push forward for ages through the dark woods, until a sudden fire washes through me—rolls along my back and through my shoulders, stealing the breath at my lips. My knees buckle and I fall at last to the cool earth.

I suppose even a living body must die in time. But I'd hoped it would last a little longer. I'd hoped for something unbroken. At least I can pass in freedom, not locked like an animal in a cage. I close my watering eyes and try to remember something better. Anything at all. The sound of summer wind along the hills, weaving its cool fingers through the sea of green that grows there. The voices of birds and spring rain and the rushing river. Anything to pull my mind away from the heaving of my lungs, the throbbing in my veins.

"*Lorëu!*"

It sounds like his voice, soft and distant, calling.

"*Lorëu!*"

A dream. It must be. A dream pulled up from some fading memory in my dying mind. A failing body's last effort to ease its passing. But the hands feel so real when they come. So warm, so gentle. And my pain eases at their touch. A good dream. Strong arms close around me, pull me close against the echo of a beating heart. A heart I recognize. I cling with the last of my strength to the shadow that holds me, this dark silhouette in my dying dream. And I want so dearly to believe it, this wonderful dream of mine.

It even smells like him.

19

"**F**ather, when did you choose a name for your son?"

They were out on the river when he asked, drifting lazily with the current. It was his father's boat. They always went down the river when the summer grew old and dusty, and the western forests were all alight with brilliant colors. Amber, orange, and golden-yellow greens. The wind always carried his favorite sort of smell when autumn came. A crisp, breezy scent. A smell full of memories.

"It was only a month before they called me to the High Seat of the House," his father told him, sitting with one arm resting along the edge of the boat and another steadying the rudder, face tipped toward the yellowing sky. "It was your mother who thought of it first."

"What does it mean, my name?"

"It comes from an old kind of speech. Words no longer spoken in the western lands."

"An ancient language?" He had been so intrigued by his father's words—leaning forward and gripping the edge of his bench, almost toppling over when the boat swayed gently beneath them. He was ten years old, that year.

"Yes, very old." His father nodded to the river then, a thin smile spreading at his lips. "*Thehlýnin*, 'my completion.' Because you completed our family, when you came."

The boy couldn't hide the pride in his face when he heard the honor of his name. Thehlýnin Dredékoldn, son of Távihn, the High Eviskyóneh of Tekéhldeth. But the glory soon faded from his mind, and the thought became suddenly overwhelming. Who was he, really?

"Father, how could I deserve such a name?"

The man at the rear of the boat with the stern jaw and strong shoulders, the man whose eyes had a way of shining like clean water, despite their dark color— the man who was his father—turned to look at him. Turned to capture the boy in his unbreaking gaze.

"Thehlýnin, if your mother gave it to you, there's no need to question. And never forget, my son, your name has another meaning. *You* are its meaning. You define it."

It was near the eight-year anniversary of his mother's death, that day on the boat. And he never did forget.

20

"Did you hear? They say another fifty were slain. Executed in a line and buried in a pile along the north wall." The man shakes his head in disdain as he speaks, taking a messy swallow from his flask and wiping his mouth with his sleeve. His older shipmate frowns at the tangled net in his hands, pulling patiently at the knots at his fingertips.

"Seems like there's more of them every time," he mumbles.

Only two days on the water. Two days, and word from the East somehow worsens. The first man runs a dirty hand through his hair, leaving the loose curls in wild array. They catch the wind like frayed feathers atop his head. He turns to the boy who sits at the end of the dock.

"Boy, did you not come from the East? Have the people of East Ataran gone mad?"

But the boy only gives a slow shrug, watching the ships as they come into the bay. The white flicker of the sails, the fishermen's shifting silhouettes, the play of the sun along the waves.

"I came from the Outlands," he tells them, not turning. "But I often heard of the great city Tekéhldeth." It's strange, the way an old life floats and fades at the edge of his young mind, threatening to bury itself in the shadows there, drifting aside but not lost, fogged but not forgotten. He could choose to let go, choose to forget. Yet three years can only heal so much.

It was his father who urged him to study the western tongue, who had hoped to take him far over the mountains to the ragged mouth of the sea—to the place where the water whips and thrashes endlessly against the black shores. His father had always hoped to live in the far west, someday. Thehlýnin has lived his father's dream and come alone to the West. A homeless refugee.

Another fifty dead, they say. Word has it the people of the East have raised themselves a king—a king to stand as judge over the famed House of East Ataran. A mighty ruler whose command cannot fail. A lord to worship. None can stand against him, though some have dared. Now they lay down their witness in the dirt beyond the north wall. Just over two hundred of them.

The thought floats old pains to the surface of the boy's mind—fleeting, flashing images he had hoped he would never recall. The black sheen of blood-soaked clothing, the crooked lines of a crazed smile—

"Well, lad, I dare say you oughtn't return to the East anytime soon," the younger man says, and he claps a heavy hand to the boy's shoulder as he climbs from the boat. "There are wicked things about."

The voice of the fisherman pulls him from the memory, jerks him like a stunned fish in the net. He's right. There is no place in the East for Thehlýnin Dredékoldn, supposed slayer of the High Eviskyóneh. Not yet.

21

I dream so deeply. I dream of crashing waves and piercing lights—of voices, near and far. Of shouting, singing, whispering. The way I dreamed in the beginning.

I dream of hot wind and swaying trees; of rain at my fingertips; of dancing, whirling prairie grasses. I dream of faces—countless, nameless faces. Faces I used to see, or have never seen. I dream until my reason is lost within me and I begin to forget the world—forgetting where to find my feet. Dreaming until I'm gasping and restless. And they wrench at the edges of my heart, these dreams. I can't hope to understand them, and despite my best efforts I'm lost in the haze of it all, drifting helplessly in the tide of wild visions. When they leave me ashore at last, I have no more thoughts to give.

My chest is heavy when I wake. Heavy like damp earth, like sagging bricks. The first breaths are ragged and wet. I cough hoarsely to clear the film.

Water!

I need it, desperately. And I can smell it—somewhere near, somewhere beyond my sight, beyond my reach. I twist and strain my stiff bones, wondering where the air has gone, pressing at the smooth layer that covers me and closes me in a cramped bundle. Am I in another sack? Am I trapped?

Stretch! Break free!

My shoulders flex instinctively, feeling strange. I manage to tear the thin sack with my foot, and the chilled night air comes bursting into my nostrils, sending a shiver along my neck. Water! The smell is stronger now, overwhelming. But my eyes won't focus.

I struggle to flop onto my stomach, clawing at the cool earth, crawling after the scent. It's difficult. I can't seem to find my hands. I try again and again to grip the grass at my face, to pull myself along, but the angle is a strain to my bones. And my arms are too *long*. Too long. . . .

I give up searching for my hands and find a way to push with my feet, pushing until the water comes to meet me. It smells like a stream. Right now, it's the most wonderful thing in the world. I fumble blindly at the shore and push into the water's cold embrace. It *is* a stream. And the current is wonderful, gliding slowly over me and soothing my stiff limbs, washing away the blood and slime and dirt.

Blood.

The scent is thick. I notice it now. What's happened to me? I didn't die, after all. Or did I? My pains have vanished. The pains that harassed me for weeks and left me breathless on the forest floor. All of it, gone.

I stretch beneath the current—stretch my arms as long as they can extend. They rise far above the water, far higher than they ought to reach. They span the width of the stream. And in a moment of unspeakable strangeness—a fleeting moment of confusion and shock and sinking realization—I find that they're no longer arms at all. My arms aren't arms anymore. They're *wings*.

I steady my feet. The water has begun to rinse the blur from my eyes. Clamoring ashore, I shake the stream from my dark feathers and blink until the image clears. Then I'm gasping, staring myself over.

Feathers!

They cover my massive wings and much of my little body, clothing me softly like a strange, shimmering coat. I try to calm my racing heart, try to dispel the wail that threatens to rise in my throat. What *am* I? What have I become? What's this dream I've fallen into?

Breathe.

I stretch my wings again, feeling a kind of swelling power in my chest that's somewhat comforting. Concentrated strength, unlike any I've ever wielded.

Wings. Breathe.

They fold nicely at my sides when I pull them in, curving backward and brushing the grass aside, sweeping gently against the ground. As far as I can tell, my head and face feel the same as usual. But my legs seem shortened . . . and is that a tail I feel?

Wings!

It's strange, and hopelessly frightening. But there must be some explanation for it all. Maybe I've died and gone to some other lifetime. Maybe I've been sleeping all along.

I look up through the canopy, searching the night sky that reveals itself in patches there. And I find it—the little cluster of lights that rests toward the western sky—the cluster that I've watched for nearly every night, from the time I first spotted it through the haze. Whatever's happened to me, or wherever I've gone, familiar stars hang overhead. Maybe I haven't gone far at all.

* * *

The sun rises to my left, when it comes. I follow the flow of the stream southward, teetering awkwardly on my new legs. I try to fool myself, try to act like I've already made sense of it all. It's almost impressive how calm I manage to remain when the morning light reveals the curled and menacing talons my feet have grown. My path leads downhill, hardening gradually beneath my steps until the dirt gives way to bare, blackened stone.

And a new echo comes to my ears. A sound from my memory. A voice I've only just learned to recognize.

Waterfall.

But it comes from below this time—the cry of the little stream as it leaps over the cliffside to the rocky bed far below. And there's the smell. The musty wetness that rises in a mist over the scene. I stand at the edge with my feet gripping the mossy rock face, eyeing the trees below and feeling the soft upsurge of wind at my chin. I was here before. I know it. Somehow, I've come back to the waterfall.

Straight ahead, the forest rolls on like a crumpled, colored blanket over the land. I could climb down, if I wanted—could wander on through the woods in search of the others. It would be a slow journey, no doubt, with these stubby legs. I can already see that they aren't built for long walks.

Walk . . .

The word sticks strangely in my mind. Somehow, it doesn't fit. I shift my shoulders, listening to the pull and flex of the muscle there, the rustle of feathers along my back. No, this body isn't meant for walking at all.

I send another glance over the cliffside, trying to swallow the sudden lump in my throat. What are these wings made for, anyway? A wild thought darts through my mind, and I find myself backing away from the rocky edge. Is this real, all of it? I take a moment to close my eyes, searching my breath for answers. I'll need to be brave.

I find a place to the west of the falls where the land begins to slump away, sliding downward to meet the lower plateau of the forest there. It's an uneven ramp—steep and littered with broken shale in places, with great boulders protruding like toothy blades from a stone river. The trees rise along the length of the rockslide, roots arching in tight bunches at their bases. I can feel the wind here. It rolls over the hillside and dances along the shale to the trees below. And the drop here is less terrifying. I crawl onto the nearest pointed boulder and find my balance, readying my shoulders, my knees.

Slowly now.

Part of me expects the wind to catch me like a dry leaf and tear me mercilessly against the stones. The rest of me is still too confused to care. I test the force of the air, letting out my wings only a hand's width from my sides. The push is gentle. Even, persistent. The wind seems to know that I hide my wings. It slides and whirls playfully along my sides, sending little tendrils through my feathers. In a moment of courage I let out my long elbows to half their full extension, and can't withhold a sharp wail when the mild gale force nearly lifts me from the stone. I pull in my limbs. I'm suddenly grateful for the gripping strength in my talon-clad feet. When did I become so light?

Slowly.

I try again, testing the angles as I move. Tilting my wings into the wind and holding them level with the earth seems to keep the air from pushing so harshly. But I'll have to let it push, eventually. Why not now?

I ease into nearly my full wingspan now, batting instinctively when the subtle gusts come against me, knees bent. Then I shift the angle of my wings and feel the air surge softly against my bones, waiting for the right moment—and the moment comes. Without thinking, I push away from the earth and beat the wind at my face. It's unlike anything I've ever known. A wonderful, wild, floating sensation. An explosion of power in my chest—like leaping into weightless water, like letting go. But I'm not sure how to let the wind carry me. I do a kind of fluttering bounce and land in the shale several paces away. The instant sends a fierce tremor through my body, and I feel my feathers rise on end.

Again!

I practice all morning long. Testing, revising. Leaping, flailing—then gliding into sloppy landings and dislodging the shale at my feet. The pieces clatter loudly as they skip and tumble down the slope. By the time the sun has crept to its high throne, I'm able to hold myself in a calm float, hovering on the wind with only an occasional steadying flap. But I don't stray far from the ground. It's like a dream—a dream long expected, yet somehow forgotten. Wasn't I meant to have wings? I can't remember now.

The afternoon finds me standing atop the falls again, waiting for the mist to settle. For the air to taste right. Waiting for this waking dream to make any sense. How have I come to this? I stare over the cliffside and try to remember who I am. But the memories are somewhere ahead of me, shifting and flickering in the open wind. Out of reach. There was a time when I knew something more about myself. Something fleeting, something old.

Like a song I once knew, or a name I once recognized.

Now, the emptiness stirs hungry circles in my lungs. And I stand with eyes wide open. The wet breath of the waterfall rises up to meet me. Stirring restlessly, inviting. I breathe it in. I'm beginning to feel it now, rising in my knees, my chest, my back. A sort of calling in the wide vaulting of the sky—a hot rhythm that weaves like excited rain in my veins. My heart begins to leap, and in a few short breaths I can scarcely hear beyond its thrumming. Suddenly, it all fits—the rhythm, the weight, the balance. It's still mine, this strange new body. And it's a strong body. Strong enough to brave the sky. Strong enough to catch the memories that float there. I'll go out to meet them.

I don't wait any longer. I crouch low before leaping from the stone and moss, opening my long wings to capture the wind, beating the air with all my might. Two—three great strokes that set my blood aflame. And the cliffside falls away below me.

Push, climb, sail! The wind becomes alive at my feather-tips, roaring at my ears, churning and channeling all around me. I rise in a southward current, welcoming the new spark in my lungs, feeling hopelessly alive. The earth shies away below, rolling out in all directions. Such a massive earth!

I'm flapping steadily now, full of racing instinct, too wild for thought. And I'm still only a few breaths from the falls when I fly into an unseen column of air. A warm wall of energy that sends me sailing sharply upward. My heart slips into my throat, and a nervous stiffening grips along my outstretched wings. I wobble in the current, twitching feathers here and there until my courage returns, tail fanned. No reason to fear. At this height my anxieties can't last. The wide horizon spreads beneath my view, and suddenly there's no room for fear in my heart—only wonder.

The sky is so tall! So remarkably high above the land! The land below—where I've crept and crawled for more days than I can number. The land where I've lived and died, dreamed and wakened. Yes, I remember that land.

I ride the rising column for a time, turning slow circles to remain in the power of its lift. Something below catches my eye only moments after I slide from the updraft and bank smoothly eastward. An odd pile of sharp shadows over the hills, rising in tortured lines along the horizon. The ruins. The grave, the labyrinth of dust and sand and ash that's framed my waking visions, holding me always in its dead and silent embrace. My home. Even at this height, I marvel at the size of the Old City—the crumbling walls, shattered rooftops, and ruined towers reaching desperately, hopelessly skyward. From my new position, their attempts seem all the more futile.

I glide without flapping, turning in an easy curve toward the north to soar over the length of the ruins. The old roads and alleys run through the rubble like the paths of insects through sand, winding and quivering in endless patterns.

Lorëu.

I find my name in the wind and turn it over in my mind. Of course that's my name. I'm still Lorëu. Always have been . . . but what does it mean for me now?

I let myself sink gradually earthward as I pass over the ruins, steadying my glide with only an occasional beat from my long wings. I'm only a leg's length away from the tallest spire when I sweep over the shining Citadel. It's just as massive from above. The sun leaps in a wide gleam from the domed rooftops, surprising my eyes and forcing me to squint.

I sail until the northern edge of the city rolls into view, marked by the slumped and vine-covered remains of a stone wall. The perfect landing place. I aim low— tail fanned wide, wings tipped almost flat against the oncoming wind as I tear my talons into the vines atop the rugged bricks. It's an awkward landing. I tip and flail to find my balance, settling at last to rest on one knee atop the wall.

And then I turn to see the place I've come to. Not far to the southwest the Citadel rises like a blurred and glowing cloud on the broken cityscape. Here, the ruins give way to an open yard where the wild grasses have spread and thrived without restraint. They rise in an odd pattern between the footstones that remain, twisting and fraying at every angle. The yard is plain, running to the distant eastern edge of the city and ending in a wide, blackened gate that stands with one iron door swung partly open—held forever in place by the rust and weeds that grow there.

There's something unusual about the earth there. I begin to walk along the ragged length of the wall for a better glimpse. There are strange, loose places in the ground—great, wide mounds of dirt that line the wall. Seven, eight, nine of them. Each wide and long enough to cover something my size four times over. Big enough for . . .

I stop just short of the first mound, feeling a cold stiffening in my throat. What is this place? I see the mounds, and a stinging memory comes back to my heart—the image of my own dark palm, held out over my sister's heaped, shallow grave.

This is the northern wall of the ruins. A place I've never before visited. A place that's beginning to choke me with its silence, to send its cold tendrils into my lungs. Something happened here, once. Something terrible. Somehow, I can feel it. I can *smell* it. And suddenly, the mounds terrify me.

I don't wait for another idea to rise in my mind. I turn and leap from the wall without giving a thought to the direction of the wind, without looking back. My heart pounds a wild melody in my ears as I climb into the air and sail high above it all—above the weeds and ruined stones. And the massive, mounded graves that lie between them.

22

It's a miracle that I find them at all. I drift for ages above the southern ruins, turning lonely circles until the sun settles in among the western mountains and lights the prairie grasses with its fading, golden hues. They're sitting in the yellow blades, toward the crest of a low hill, when I see them. Watching the west, hardly moving at all. There's no wind when I come down in the tall grass, not far from where I spotted them. Like the land and all its livings things are holding their breath, waiting to see what this strange new flying creature is like. I find myself wondering along with them.

The two of them come walking to meet me, the sun's dying light reflected in their wide eyes—lit like four yellow moons in the evening air. Then they stand motionless before me, staring. It's strange, the way my memory jolts to life at the sight of them, the way my identity becomes something more tangible in my mind when I see the faces of my friends. I fold my wings, breathe the last of the sunshine-air that hangs among the grass. For a time, all is still.

Ilith is the first to take another step toward me, her mouth falling softly open. I marvel silently at how tall she seems to me now. I must've shrunk. She drifts to a stop several paces away, wrinkling her white forehead.

"Loreü?" The whisper scarcely crosses the space between us.

I bite my lip, give her a nod. The tears come from nowhere, leaking out and wetting the dark plume on my neck. For some reason, I'm helpless to stop them.

"Were you . . . reborn?" she asks.

"I . . . I don't know," I tell her.

* * *

The daylight fades swiftly. There was a time when we would have slept in the open grass. Now we scramble for shadows when evening comes. We spend the night at the edge of the hills, tucked beneath the fallen beams of a slumping garden house. Ekyán slides in first, and I follow close behind—merely bowing my head where the others are forced to crouch down. The moonlight slips in between the cracks, its pale fingers falling like little pillars in the shadows.

I'm not sure how to sleep. My folded wingtips brush along the ground as I kneel, and lying on my back just wouldn't work. My first night as an eagle. Ilith watches my awkwardness for a moment, then settles down with her back to the mess of bricks and wood behind us.

"We'll sit up with you," she says. Ekyán does the same. I fit comfortably between them, and discover suddenly that any dusty pile of bricks can seem like home, the moment my good friends are beside it. Beside *me*.

"They didn't hurt you, did they?" Ekyán speaks at last. I look at him, shake my head.

"One of them let me go," I tell him. Ilith wasn't listening. She folds her skinny arms, lets her eyes fall shut.

"It's good that you found us today. We're not thinking to linger around here much longer," she breathes.

"You plan to leave for good?"

Her eyes slide partly open again, and she stares out to the grass that rises up as a shaded curtain beyond the edge of our hiding place.

"The ruins are becoming strange," she says. And then we are silent. I don't question. I don't need to.

They're both asleep long before I am. My new body is restless. I lean into Ilith's shoulder and try to remember how to sleep, try to remember how I did this before. When did today begin? I close my eyes, let the images float and flutter over me until my mind is too weary to consider it all. Dripping feathers, slick stones on the banks of the stream, sunlight scattered over the ruins far below me . . . and a line of dark mounds in an empty yard—I open my eyes, breathing the dry dust in the air, trying desperately to think of anything else. The mounds terrify me.

"The ruins are becoming strange."

Strange. The ruins are becoming strange . . . strange. . . . I'm so exhausted. But there's a buzzing in the back corners of my mind, and I can't seem to hide it away. Something I've almost forgotten, something that fights for the last thread of strength in my mind. A memory, a word. A word. . . .

"The others don't know. They don't understand your speech."

The voice comes back to me, and suddenly I'm sitting entirely upright, awake and hopelessly aware of the thrumming in my chest.

One of them let me go! One of them *spoke* to me— spoke such confusing things, such jumbled words— how had I forgotten? I try to remember the moment, to think past the fear and pain that scar my memory. There was a word, a word that itched in my mind, a word that was whispered in through the wooden slats of that box where they kept me.

"In the ruins, a month ago . . ."

I hunch over, touch my head to my boney knees, remembering the bite of the rope at my wrists.

". . . just you . . . and he was a big man."

Man. He spoke of the Creature that attacked me, so long ago, outside the Citadel. Man. The figure that stood watching on the Avenue, when Kehlvi was dying. The monster that threw the spear. The dark figures that took me from the waterfall, that took me to their camp with the smells and the smoke and the terrible shadows. Man. The Creature who set me free. They're of Man, all of them. I've seen Man.

It's the word that first came to me when I went alone to the Citadel, searching for Thayl. But until now, it failed to make any connections in my mind. I toss it in my head, testing the weight of it, the way it tips and balances in my memories. Where does it fit? I knew Man once, long ago. I can feel it. There was a time when Man was ordinary to me—when I had no questions, no doubts, no fears. Somehow, I know it. Évrieth knew it. But where does it fit?

I shake my head, ruffling the thick feathers along my neck and shoulders, feeling in circles around the word that plagues me. I've seen Man, but not his face. Maybe I will, someday. Someday, when all the answers come back to me.

23

It's raining softly when he comes to the western fields again. The fields where the people of the outer limits have always raised their hedges and little gardens. Even now, he can smell the sweet blossoms growing there, just over the next hill. He stands empty handed, no coat to keep the rain from slicking his sleeves to his skin—from misting his hair until it lies like dark silk over his ears. It begins to run in little rivers down his neck. But he doesn't notice.

The city rises like a dim and sullen cloud in the midmorning haze, shifting and vanishing in places where the rain is lost to mist. There was always such dense fog when the rain came. . . .

Eight years. Eight years spent far away. And now he's here again, staring into the city of his childhood. The city he once left behind. The city his father never escaped. He stands for ages in the western fields, watching the way his memories float up with the fog and mingle between the distant towers—the way they billow and curl like clouds over the walls, the spires, the rooftops.

Somehow, the city has brought him back—reeled him in from afar. It pulled him in the way the fishermen of the West would pull. Jerking, tugging relentlessly. And he came—came as a weary fish in the cords, hopeless and helpless and lost. And now that he has come, the son of the eighty-first Eviskyóneh has no idea what to become. Or how to live.

The hills swell up on both sides of the road as he shuffles toward the empty outer lanes of the city—pressing in on him, waving wet prairie grasses in his face. Green walls that shut out the misty fields beyond. He follows the path until it slumps and weaves beneath an arched, mossy bridge. It's a low and narrow roof, but at least it can keep the rain from pattering along his head and shoulders. The air is colder than he remembers, in the East. And more silent, beyond the soft thrumming of the rain.

There was a time when all the city could be heard beyond the rain. Such silence now. For a moment, it almost grips him. He shivers, unable to shake the awful sinking that swells inside. A desperate feeling, like the city awaits him—lies in soundless expectation for the return of the boy who abandoned it. Waiting for its chance to reclaim him. Maybe they'll find him. Maybe they're still looking. Maybe they know. Why has he come back to this place?

An echo comes hiccupping down the path, then—a wet, steady slapping in the mud. The sound of wrapped shoes in the rain. A city dweller, coming along the lane. A girl. Probably somewhere near his own age, or younger. She comes with her head ducked beneath a wide hood, walking with her arms tucked away into the folds of her shawl. She comes to the bridge and pauses beneath it, raising her head to watch the rain before she notices the stranger beside her. And she gasps softly.

"Didn't see you there," she murmurs.

They sound so smooth, so fluid, the old words. Like waves in a slow river. The language of his memories. He isn't sure how to respond, and tries to make a friendly face. It's a pathetic attempt.

"Are you here to listen as well?" She raises her voice to be heard over the rain. The rain that begins to beat and slap angrily against the cobble. It frightens the muddy puddles and sends them thrashing and splattering along the stones.

"To the rain?" He's surprised at the thinness of his own voice. How long has he gone without speaking?

"The thunder," she corrects him. She slides the hood from her head and bats the brown curls from her face. He shrugs loosely, trying to remember how to behave.

"Have you heard any yet?" he asks her. She smiles mildly in reply.

"Only once, so far," she tells him, and he can hear the patient anticipation in her voice. The rain seems to raise its loud music then, hoping desperately to join in on their words. Thehlýnin allows himself a sigh.

"The weather's about as wet as I remember it," he tells the mud.

"You're a visitor, then?" The girl slips her hands into her shawl again, eyes raised to the shaded sky. What's the answer? The words mix and tangle in his mouth, threatening to slide out all at once. Or not at all. His thoughts rise in a flurry, searching vainly for the answer. But he doesn't know the answer. And it's such an empty feeling.

The thunder comes then, starting its low rumble somewhere far away, beyond the clouds, the rain, the city. Then it bellows from its hiding place and sends a subtle trembling through the hills—cackling and tumbling toward the south. And a wild grin spreads along the girl's pale face.

24

Is that a storm lying over the southern trees? I tip on the wind for a better glimpse and feel the currents pressing me into the curve. It *is* a storm. A bulbous pile of dark shades, rolling and tumbling in the air. I can see the rain from here. It stretches down to the earth in gray sheets. Silent, and somehow motionless—stuck like wide stripes of dried paint in the dulling sky. But the wind moves eastward. Maybe the rain will never reach us.

They wave their arms on the hillside below to signal me, and I see the excitement in their shrunken, rapid motions. I've followed them to a place along the edge of the woods, separated from the southeast end of the Old City by only a few windswept hills. Then there are others. Five, eight—fifteen of them come rushing out from the shade of the trees, raising their hands to shade their eyes, faces turned skyward. Six more appear in the crowd as I'm tilting my wings into a slow break. Do they all need to watch? I'm still not very stable with my landings.

I come to a hopping stop just beyond the place where Ilith stands, and the crowd comes shuffling slowly toward us, all gasps and whispers. There are many of them. More survivors gathered together than I've seen for months. And there are old faces among them—faces I haven't seen since our days in the orchard. Faces that vanished the night of Kehlvi's death.

"You found them—the others," I breathe, extending my left wing to Ilith's leg beside me, forgetting that there's no hand at the end of it. "Do they . . . have you taught . . . ?"

"Yes, they've all learned hitérian," she tells me. "The newcomers have practiced moving energy since our first week together."

I turn to catch her gaze.

"Week?"

She glances to the others, then back to me again.

"Yes, Lorëu. You were gone for three," she tells me plainly. *Three weeks?* The crowd reaches us then, before I have a chance to marvel. They all try to talk at once, shaking their heads in disbelief, blinking their wide eyes over and over again.

"Wings!"

"How could—?"

"Did it hurt?"

"But what about your hands?"

"Did the monsters do this to you?"

"Will you ever change back?"

Their questions pour out in a jumble—until all the words have fallen useless in the grass. Until the utter lack of answers catches up to us. And then we are all silent. Wordless and exhausted. I look up into their multicolored faces and try to find something useful in my memory, something satisfying to tell them. But I'm as lost as they are. And I can't seem to stop searching among them, sifting through the faces for the one I need, the one that isn't here. A dark face. I swallow.

"The Creatures didn't do anything to me," I tell them, and I hear the wind singing over us. "I don't know what happened to me. All I can tell you is, it seems . . . natural."

Someone comes pressing through the crowd then. A little golden-brown speckled boy I've come to love. But now he stands half a head above my own shrunken stature. He reaches out his hand, lets only the tips of his thin fingers meet the edge of my feathers before pulling back again, wide eyed.

"Lorëu," he whispers, "can I become an eagle too?" I see the trembling in his glassy stare. The others have frozen all around me—breath halted, eyes fixed, waiting. Just beyond my shoulder, I catch Ilith's hard gaze. It's the question we all seem to have. I look back to the boy.

"Maybe, Saiven. Maybe everyone can, someday."

* * *

They find so many names for my new shape, over the next handful of days. The bird, the flier, the feather-full, the changed one. But one name seems to stick above the others: *virít*, "the big eagle."

I continue to experiment with my new body. I spend hours in the air—climbing, soaring, banking, and diving. I learn to hover on the high winds while I watch the ground below; to recover smoothly from tumbles and stalls; to fly slowly, with only the softest motion in my feathers, not far over the heads of my friends. I find that the soles of my feet have become powerful contact surfaces for hitérian. With Ekyán's help, I learn to dive in from above and pull the energy from the spines of boars and rodents before the poor animals can think to run. My wonder only grows the more I learn. And it all seems so right, so natural.

"I think our bodies are meant to change like this, Ilith. But for some reason, we've forgotten," I call down to her from my place on a high bough. We've practiced all morning and caught enough to feed ourselves for the next seven days. She's lying on her back in the shade below, looking up to the canopy beyond both our heads.

"But how did it happen?" she calls back.

"I don't know yet, but I think the change started ages ago. It started with the pains I had in my joints." I shift my shoulders, remembering the stiffness.

"That's related?"

"The pain was at its worst just before I lost consciousness," I tell her, "and it was gone when I woke." Down below, she makes a frown and tips her chin to stare at something new.

"So, what made it start?" Never satisfied.

I try to think back, try to trace the pains to some logical point. The path is crumbled and confused in my mind. But I don't stop searching. I toss my memories around all afternoon, searching through them over and over in my head until I could rehearse them in my sleep. It's not the first time we've done something new, something we can't understand. But last time it was so much simpler. Last time, it was only a matter of moving energy. And I did it at my own will. This is something different. This is something so much more.

It's near sunset, two days later, when the answer comes floating softly to my mind. We're settling in for the evening—shifting energy back and forth to help one another climb into the safety of the trees before nightfall. Evening. The time when I always miss him most. And I'm thinking of him when the answer comes. Thayl. He was there in the beginning, when the days were still dark with ash and fog and haze. He was there when Évrieth walked with us, when the first Creature found us, and when I first discovered hitérian. And it was Thayl who reversed hitérian, who somehow taught the energy to generate within my bones, with a single touch of his hands to my back. A moment we have yet to replicate. And now, as I find a thick branch for my overnight perch, the memory suddenly captures me. I've revisited that moment in the Citadel countless times before. But now it clings to the front of my mind, and I can't seem to pull it away. The facts roll through my head all over again. He didn't take; he *gave*. Give, take, give, take. I turn the scene over, try to remember the way the fiery energy washed over me that day. The way it burned into my blood, my breath.

"Ilith!" My whisper is coarse and nasty. I'm suddenly too thrilled to control it. Her white face appears, peeking down from several branches above.

"What? Are you stuck?"

"No!" I almost scowl. "Come down here. I think I've just found something!"

She comes slinking down from several branches above, crawling with her red sash tied snugly around her shoulders. She drops onto my bough and squats with a sigh on her breath, hunching in the dim light before me.

"If it's a beetle again—"

"Ilith, the *ek'let'eh*, the change! I think I know what started it, what made me the virít!" If I had ordinary arms, I'd be flinging them in the air. Ilith blinks.

"You . . . you have?" Her eyes have missed the last rays of the sun, gone from spring-green to darker, mossy tones.

"It was Thayl. He somehow taught me to generate my own strength—to build energy from within. And in the process it must have . . . must have triggered something!" My wings fan out excitedly, and I teeter— almost losing my grip on the bark at my feet. Ilith ducks beneath the mass of flailing feathers to raise her arm like a securing fence beside me.

"Careful!" she chides. "And what do you mean? You think reversed hitérian somehow turns us into eagles?"

I calm down, set my thoughts in order.

"Ilith, maybe it doesn't have to," I tell her. "Maybe this time was an accident. He didn't know what he was doing."

"But if we mean it to, it *could*?" A faraway look has come into her face. We're thinking together now. There's a moment of silence, and I can almost hear the slow churning in our heads. The sound of something wonderful rising at the edges of our minds, just beyond our reaching fingers. I stare at the curling, twisting patterns in the bark beneath us.

"Maybe it's something to do with the way the hands are placed," Ilith murmurs. The thought catches me.

"You might be right," I wonder aloud. "Until that day, I'd never *received* hitérian, only *taken*. And not in my back—only my arms, my hands. . . ."

As soon as the idea comes, it feels right. My heart starts to leap and thrum in its place. Ilith looks up then, eyes wide enough to capture the reflection of my entire body in their circular frames. She raises her hand in the air between us, about to say something more, maybe searching for the right words—

But she's interrupted. Our thoughts are cut short by a sound unlike any I've ever heard. A wild, piercing wail—a harrowing cry that rises up and rings over the hills, crashing like lightning in the trees and shaking the blood in our veins. A scream that cuts the wind and thrashes horribly in our ears before it falls and chokes itself to silence. It came from the north. From the ruins. And all the sounds of our camp come to silence after it. We all heard it. The entire *world* must have heard it. Sitting beside Ilith, I turn to stone. An eternity passes over us. A soundless, motionless moment of crippling horror. And when I find the strength to move my head at last, I can't speak. Neither can Ilith. With effort, she finds her arm at last and motions upward. I nod stiffly in response.

I don't care to wonder what might have caused it. Not now, when the night is coming on, when the woods are so still and shadowed. Not ever, really. And so we climb. We'll all sleep higher in the trees tonight.

25

It's a comfortable home. Warm, and apart from the ruckus of the inner avenues. A place where he's dared to walk with his head uncovered in the heat of the day. He's stayed three nights here, in their little house at the corner of one of the western outer lanes. They're kind enough to let him stay. Kind in a way that often leaves Thehlýnin marveling subtly to himself. After all, he's little more than a stranger to them. Three nights, and already they treat him as if he were some long-absent son returned from a heroic journey— insisting that he join them by the fire each evening, asking him again and again to share the stories of the West. Three nights, and Thehlýnin finds himself almost at ease, in the city of his childhood.

It's a calm evening, and the fireside conversation has lulled itself to silence. He rises from his seat by the fire, donning a loose hood as he reaches to throw the latch on the door.

"What are you doing?" She's caught him by the wrist, a low and anxious edge in her voice that he doesn't expect. Her words have been so light and warm since three mornings before, when she found him in the rain—somehow full of spark and cheer and wonder despite the growing tension in the city streets. Tonight is different, and it's almost startling. But even now he can hear the softness that still lingers there, pressing behind the quickness of her words. The subtle tone of genuine concern.

"Just out for a walk," he tells her. He's pulled the door just beyond the threshold, allowing only a sliver of night to spread along its edge. Darkness has fallen. But the air is still warm.

"You ... you can't." She glances to the blackness as she whispers. The blackness that awaits beyond the bolts and chains that line the doorframe. In the room behind her, the others remain silent. And there's a kind of expression in their faces that's difficult to name. Something unspoken. Something like terror. But the kind of terror that people try to bury in their stomachs. What have they seen?

He tries to find the right question to ask, but the words don't come. And so he says nothing at all. He takes his hand from the door, and the girl reaches past him to push it softly closed.

"No one goes out when the night comes," she says, and she looks up into his eyes for just an instant. "Not anymore."

26

We're going to need rope. It takes them all far too long to come down to the forest floor when morning returns. They cling so nervously to the thick bark, sharing strength to lengthen their grips. And I don't blame them. Wings make some things so much simpler. Watching from below, I stand ready to leap up and catch them under the arms with my feet or ankles, if they fall. But none of them do.

I like to think that our time as a frail and dying race is coming to an end, now that we've mastered the first form of hitérian. But only one of us has managed to unlock the second. And I alone have enjoyed the benefit. Unlike me, my friends and fellow survivors are still forced to live from one energy exchange to the next. And until we can change that, climbing tall trees will be a challenge.

The early afternoon sun is only beginning to tip the shadows of the trees when we gather together.

"All right, all right. I'll go too. But I say we make it as quick as possible, traveling in groups. Only heading for the places we're certain of. Where we *know* we've seen rope before." Ilith takes her usual authoritative pose as she speaks, bringing her hands to her sides and keeping her shoulders even, jaw tight. It was her idea to hold a meeting. "I don't want to lose anyone."

The rest of us loosely agree, nodding our heads and fiddling with the leaves at our feet. Across the circle, a silvery-gray-colored boy raises his voice.

"Five of us have seen a place—up toward the northwestern edge, where there were ropes tangled and hanging all over a fallen wall. I remember the way," he says.

"And there are the ropes at the docks, along the river," I add, shifting my shoulders and inadvertently brushing someone's nearby ankle with my left wingtip. "They hold the old boats in place."

"Two small groups, then. One to the city and one to the river," someone says.

"Back here before sunset," another chimes, and the circle lets out a collective murmur of approval. We're all turning into the trees and dispersing in several directions when Ilith appears beside me.

"We're going north with Lotánehl," she tells me.

"Then I'll join you," I reply. "The river isn't far from here. Let the younger group take that. I can fly all over the city and leave the ropes in a pile for you at the southern gate."

Ilith pulls her attention away from the others in order to offer me the full intensity of her glare.

"Didn't you hear what I said?" she presses. "You want to go alone? How can we be sure you'll meet us there?"

"I've already got a few places in mind," I assure her. "Don't worry. It won't take long."

And it doesn't. I've crossed over the ruins and gathered three decent cords to the hill outside the crumbling southern gate before the others have started back with their load.

I save the largest rope for last. I spot it as I come in a slow curve from the west, gliding just high enough to pass over the jagged peaks of the southern Old City. The Avenue looks almost bigger from above. And when I come down to the broken, ash-veiled pavement, I marvel at the sight of it all. The scorched and crumbling bricks, the crushed and tattered awnings, the subtle haze of dust and old soot stirring along the gasps of the wind—all as they've always been, but different.

Looking east, I glimpse the swaying tips of the orchard trees, rising beyond the blended hues of the rubble. Everything's the same . . . but it's changed, hasn't it? I frown to myself. I was dying when I first stood here. All of us were. Dying, and knowing nothing but the collapse and ruin all around us. No, the Avenue hasn't changed at all. But *we* have. And all the world is beginning to look different to me now.

The rope is twisted and knotted among the remains of a fallen wooden structure. For a moment, I stand eyeing it. How can I manage this alone, with only my feet to work with? I leap and land with a flutter atop one of the biggest knots, digging my claws into the fat coil. There's no way to fly away with this. Not while it's so tangled and woven into the surrounding bricks and splintered boards. And its weight is surprising. I'll likely be forced to drag it with short, low-level flights. A slow and tiring solution. But it's possible.

I'm clawing at the knots and tangles, beating my wings in an effort to pull them loose, when I become subtly aware of an odd numbness in the air. A crawling, compressed sensation. It begins in my stomach, climbs like cold static along my spine, my shoulders— something I've felt before. A feeling like blackness. Blackness that can't be seen.

Now the breath is stopped in my throat, choked behind the sudden tightness of my teeth. I give up on the rope and drop to the broken pavement, suddenly too stiff to fold my wings entirely. Too stiff to do anything but stand staring down at the wide mouth of the Avenue—at the motionless figure that now exists there. It hangs on the air, blurred and strange, like a painted echo on the afternoon breeze. A shaded, faded image. The image of a man. Only a short distance away, a few leaps north from my position. Close enough for me to see the tallness of its stature, the real and solid light of its peering eyes—such burning, shining points of light. The sight of it somehow cements me like a brick in dried plaster, stifling the terrified wail that tries to escape my chest. The blackness is suffocating. And the image begins to change. Its long arms begin to rise. Rising, rising. Lifting steadily until they've risen high over the figure's clouded head. A wide, triumphant spread in the air. And something happens to the face. An awful, wrinkling, spreading movement. Is it . . . a grin? A broad, horrible grin that sends a jarring through my bones—

I turn to the southwest without another thought. Leaping into the air, I beat the wind with all the strength my little body can hope to give, struggling to pull the breath into my cold lungs. Tears well up at the edges of my eyes and blur the sight of the land below, running in chilled streams along the sides of my face.

It was the same. The same presence that found us in the Citadel, that stood waiting at the red doors when I returned there alone. The same blackness that took my dearest friend away. My mind is all racing thoughts; all screaming instinct; all rushing, tangled memories. Somehow, the blackness has found and torn at the knot in my head. The knot that locks away something ancient inside me, dreams lost or forgotten. And as I fly, my mind slips abruptly away—falls into some vivid scene that rises from the backside of my thoughts. And then I'm no longer rising on the wind, but standing. Standing in a place more grand and spectacular than any I've ever dared to imagine. A place with golden towers and shining banners, with vibrant sashes of every color, with bells and bright metals and giant flames hanging overhead. Standing in an endless sea of faces—people, like me—all staring at the man who rises above the rest. A man whose countenance sears and radiates like the rays of the setting sun, whose robes shine and shimmer like the light of dusk on the river's face. A man whose eyes burn like churning flames. And when he speaks with lifted hands, all the people are caught in the terrible ringing of his voice. A voice that sets a horrible twisting in my stomach. And it plants a kind of fear in my soul that I'm hopeless to describe.

It's a miracle that I'm somehow able to remain airborne. The vision jolts like static through my mind, and when it throws me back into the present I find myself flying blindly westward along the city's edge.

A vision, a dream!

I try to shake the trembling from my mind, try to convince myself that I simply imagined it all. But even as I strain to push the images away, I'm hopeless to stem the cold rush of dread that leaks into my heart. The dread that the vision is somehow woven into my reality, threatening to overtake me and to come to life before my eyes.

No! Just a dream, a dream. . . .

* * *

I spot the others just beyond the southern end of the ruins, at the start of the hills. Ilith comes to meet me as I glide down, and I can already see the concern in her face. How does she know?

"What's happened?" she calls to me, swatting the tall grass from her path. But I don't answer at first. My voice is caught somewhere deep in my lungs. And searching for it only makes my throat feel tighter. She reaches me and searches all over my feathered frame, searching for anything out of place. The others appear behind her now, glancing wordlessly to one another.

"Lorëu, what's happened? Are you hurt?" She squats to look directly into my eyes, and I can see my own wet face shining back at me.

"I—I left the last rope," I realize aloud, and I look from side to side, as if I might find it lying around.

"Lorëu!"

I look back into Ilith's waiting gaze, try to calm the subtle tremors that still quake in my bones.

"It was . . . I saw it. I saw it again. It found me there," I tell her. Her eyes dart back and forth to catch each of mine. And they widen.

"What do you mean? One of those giant Creatures?"

I shake my head. "The—the thing . . . the thing that found us in the Citadel. I saw it. In the street."

Ilith only wrinkles her forehead, and I can see the ideas whirring behind her eyes. I hadn't noticed Lotánehl kneeling to my right. His silver-gray color has almost allowed him to slip into the shadows between the tall blades of the prairie grasses.

"You saw the figure?" He scarcely whispers above the rustling of the grass. I turn to look at him.

"You—you've seen it too?" I stammer. Ilith and Ekyán look as surprised as I probably do. The wind has risen now. It bats at the fur atop their heads and shoulders, leaving random puffs standing on end. And the chill of it makes my feathers rise.

"Only once," he tells me.

27

That night, we all agree to leave the Old City forever. Something strange has come to the ruins. Something none of us can name or explain. We'll find a new home for ourselves. It's something we should've done long ago—and *would* have, if we had learned hitérian sooner.

The trees grow taller in the south, where the land shifts from calm, grassy hills to red cliffs and wooded mountains. I've glimpsed it, from the sky. We can follow the river. There's a place not more than a long day's walk from our current camp, where the greater flow is joined by a small and fast-flowing stream from the east. There the water gathers strength and begins to toss and thrash along its way. The river becomes angry, to the south. And it must lead somewhere—maybe to a place too far away to know the darkness and destruction that haunts us here.

We don't delay our departure. We leave as soon as our numbers are confirmed, when the stars have only begun to peer through the violet evening haze that hangs over the trees. And we travel long into the night. My people creep wearily through the thick shadows of the trees, pausing only now and then to find their breaths and listen to the sleeping woods. Circling in the wind above, I can scarcely spot the subtle shifting of their shapes. They vanish at times, as the light of a single partial moon wanes and fades behind midnight clouds.

We're within the voice of the narrow stream when we settle for the deepest hours of the night. They signal me with the wave of a bright sash near the treetops. Whoever managed it has climbed impressively high. The trees in these dark woods are the tallest I've seen.

I sail down through the canopy to find Ilith and Ekyán already coiling their ropes, settling in the arms of a broad tree a little apart from the rest. Securing ropes, wedging water satchels, tying canvases. Our new routine. We sleep in the medium-high perches, where the boughs are still thick and wide enough to let us lie comfortably. Lately, it seems natural to me—sleeping with my talons gripped into the thick bark and my wings folded loosely at my sides. But tonight sleep comes to me in random, uneven doses. The air is too strange, tonight. Too sharp. And I can't seem to put away the noise in my head. A subtle buzzing, like a nightfly flitting just beyond my hearing. After what feels like hours of restless thoughts, I decide to give up on sleep.

Someone's sitting awake in the lower boughs, when I open my eyes. Ilith. She sits with her shoulders hunched over her knees, facing away. But I can recognize her white fur from anywhere. And the red sash that lies in thick folds across her back. I wait a moment before leaning toward the slow-curving edge of my branch.

"You awake too?" I whisper, somewhat surprised at the lack of coarseness in my voice. I'm so exhausted. Below, Ilith twitches her ears softly backward at the sound of my words. But she doesn't move. Why is she perched so far below? It's too low. . . .

"Ilith?" I whisper. Somewhere nearby in the night, a subtle rustling whips and toys with the leaves, then dies away again. "Is something wrong?" The question falls awkwardly in the air, hangs like wet moss from the branches that surround us. I can feel it now. I didn't need to ask. I can see the fear in her outline before my words are finished. A sort of stiffness that turns her frame to hard lines—a stillness that snatches up the Ilith I know and hides her away, turns her into something full of panicked instinct. Something more capable of fear. I try to hush the soft flutter that rises in my heart.

"Ilith," I breathe. "Ilith, climb higher. Come to this br—" I catch sight of something through the leaves, and the words dissolve at my teeth before they can finish. There's something there, standing on the forest floor below. Something solid—tall but crooked, swaying slightly on its feet. A hulking silhouette I've come to recognize. My stomach drops.

Fly!

The impulse bursts in my bones—I want to yell, to snatch Ilith's arm in my claws and pull her up into the sky, pull her to safety.

Fly!

I want to shrink into the dark places of the canopy, fold away into the leaves where the nightmares can never find us. But I can't. And instead I'm left motionless, frozen by the sight of the swaying figure below, too terrified to blink the wetness from my eyes. Ilith is too low. And it knows.

The scene erupts too quickly—like a black and silent dream, a horrible jumbling of motion and shadow and muffled sound. The man lurches suddenly forward, leaping at our tree—and then I'm in the air, wrestling my wings through the branches, clawing madly toward the shoulders of the beast that's somehow pulled my friend to the ground. Ilith scrambles along the forest floor ahead, struggling to find her feet—the monster stomping at her heels, wide hands swiping at the air, the leaves, the bushes. It feels its way through the shadows, stumbling like a blind and rabid creature. A *mindless* creature. But it's moving fast. Purposefully. I meet its pace and bring my talons down onto its neck, tearing skin and sapping energy, then topple backward when it rises up to let out a loud, tormented cry—identical to the one we heard rising from the ruins several nights ago. It's a horrible wail that jars my heart and starts a ringing in my ears. Ekyán appears from the shadows above and slips past me to steal the strength of the man-creature's massive legs. It falls forward onto its knees, but doesn't give up the chase—crawling and groping wildly at the ground before it. I'm coming down on its arm when the beast closes a massive fist around my leg. In the other it clutches a fallen branch. And Ekyán turns to intercept—but there's no time. I scream.

"EKYÁN!"

He cries out when the coarse branch is raked across his side, and I see him shrink down into the leaves. But Ilith has turned back and pulled him up before I can attempt to respond. She moves away with desperate speed, Ekyán limping awkwardly with her support. I manage to kick and claw my way free, using one foot to weaken my captor's grasp on the other. I pull the hot energy from the beast's back, and it collapses with hardly a gasp to the cool earth, still grabbing violently at the weeds that grow there, despite being powerless to lift itself again. And then I sail through the trees, spreading my wings where I can, leaping and gliding over logs and stones. Fleeing southwest, toward the sound of the stream. Toward the sound of Ilith's wavering voice. I find them at the water's edge.

"Ekyán, we can do this, you hear? Listen to me." She cradles him in her arms, pulling the sash from her shoulder to wrap it tightly around his torn and bleeding side. He only breathes in reply, blinking over and over again. I land beside her, heart in my throat. It's a familiar scene—the blood, the fear. The sort of sight I've long hoped to forget. But this time is different. I can feel it. I *know* it.

Ilith turns to me. Her eyes are red and trembling, but not wet. "We need to try," she says. "Help me hold him."

I open my wing and bring Ekyán's head to my shoulder. I'm the perfect height. Ilith kneels close beside us, pressing her thin hands to her brother's back, searching. If only I had my arms. I do my best to close my dark wings around them both, to shelter us all from the fear of the night. From the thought of losing anyone.

Breathe. . . .

Ilith lets her hand rest along Ekyán's spine, eyes closed. And then something happens. It starts with Ilith. I can feel it where her arm leans against my side—a deep surge that rises and flows in the tendons there. I close my eyes and trace the motion. Listening to it, breathing with it. My memory stirs, and the image of a dark hand gripping my arm comes to mind. Along with the echo of my own voice.

"Can you feel it?"

I can. Hitérian, just as we've come to know it. But it isn't the same, not entirely. This time, it flows *outward*. We can move it—shift the energy the way we learned to do long ago. But it's become something new, something to *give*.

The motion is effortless, natural. I sense the energy beginning to slide from Ilith's hands and into Ekyán. And then to me. I feel it rising as a subtle wave in the deepest center of my chest. A burning, a rippling. An electric pulse—a churning swell of energy that rises up from our bones. I focus on it, feel it shifting, then follow the flow—send my own strength surging outward, radiating from my heart and shoulders. Ilith stirs and gasps beside me as the current passes back through her, and all at once I feel the tension fall away from Ekyán's quaking shoulders. Somehow, we become a circle of energy. We sense it together—rising, coursing through our bones, burning through the locks we placed there, sewing life into the breath, the sinews. We shift it together in rhythm, sending it coursing from heart to hand, to back, to shoulder, and through the heart again. Through each of our hearts. It's wonderful, miraculous—and I can hardly believe that we've done it. We've found it at last.

28

The streets of Tekéhldeth have changed. The smells, the colors, the sounds. There are men with blades and golden sashes in the streets, standing at every corner, every alley-mouth. There are yellow banners hanging—blanketing the high walls, the tunnels, and the arches in the lanes. Shining banners covered in words of praise and adoration, of admonition and declaration.

The Glory of His Eye Shall Lead You!

Lord of the Voice Presides Forever!

Traitors Cannot Stand!

The banners talk of the High Directing Hand. The magnificent king who has come to heal the sickness of the people, to succor the wounds of the Ten Regions. The Savior of East Ataran. And of the West as well. And one day, the lands beyond the sea—when all the people shall come to know his glory. Or so they say, in the streets. The longer Thehlýnin wanders among them, the more he wonders if the people here could survive saying anything else.

There was once an open lane in the far eastern district of the city where the prophets and the politicians would stand on their high stools and shout their wisdom into the crowds. A place where voices cracked and opinions flew like dust and hot smoke in the air. Now, there's only the barracks. When did the soldiers of Tekéhldeth become so many? So severe? There's no rest, in the city. The people hurry along the paved ways with heads bowed and shawls tightly wrapped, visiting only the shops they absolutely must.

Only the outer lanes know any silence, any peace—where the water flows in little channels and gathers in ponds beside the road. Nearly nine years have passed now, since the fall of the eighty-first Eviskyóneh. And at twenty-three years old, Thehlýnin can scarcely bear to see the face that peers out of the water at him. The mask of a solemn, dark-eyed man. The face of his father.

*　*　*

"Come, something's happened." She uses the speech of the West, when she finds him wandering the outer lanes, away from the crowds. Words he taught her. Her tight curls are tousled around her face, when he looks. She cut them short only several days ago.

"Something bad?" He reaches to feel for his hood as he turns toward her, making certain it's still hanging there. She shakes her head.

"I don't know," she says, "but all the city has gone to the southern steps of the House to see it."

The Grand Way is a sea of heads, when they reach it—a wide and colorful river that stirs and lashes up at the walls and the pillars, where the people have climbed for better views. Despite the brightness of the midday sun, the greatest of the high torches are lit, and they rise in pairs along the length of the Way—pouring orange and golden hues from their magnificent dishes. Like great bowls of fire.

"We'll see nothing from here!" the girl shouts, straining to be heard over the pressing crowds. Thehlýnin shakes his head in agreement beneath his hood, then motions toward the north. They turn into the surrounding alleys and weave northward through the commotion, following alongside the Grand Way until they come almost to the wide and majestic front columns of the House. There they manage to climb onto the steps of an old inn balcony and slip into a high place beneath the eaves, where the people have packed themselves like cattle against the wooden rails. The sound of the city is almost bursting their ears. Chattering, shouting, clapping, and yelling. But Thehlýnin has scarcely found sure footing against the wall of the inn when the commotion comes to a sudden halt, and all the eyes of the crowd are turned to the steps of the House. The abrupt silence is startling. Almost stifling.

And then the man can be seen, beyond the marble steps—given away by the golden glow that precedes him. A radiant light that floods the hall and paints the pillars before him. He comes like a king from between the pillars of the House, walking barefoot, draped in long, glimmering, marvelous robes. He comes like a god. Beside him, somehow suspended in the air, floats a tall and shining rod—like the staff of an emperor, full of intricate lines and colors that shift and shimmer at every angle. Orange and yellow light leaps and streams from the man's presence, settling like a warm flame all about him, and the light of his eyes is sharp and terrible. But not so terrible as the smile that spreads along his face—a perfect, horrible grin that chokes the breath of the son of the eighty-first Eviskyóneh. A grin the boy has seen before.

The sea of faces in the Grand Way remains transfixed beneath its ruler's gaze—too lost, too terrified to react. But then the god raises his arms high into the air, into a triumphant spread to the sky, and all the city erupts in mindless applause. They salute him, though their hearts are fainting in their chests.

"At last, my people, I reveal to you my glory! Behold your Guide!" His voice rushes and resonates over the heads of the people, rings with such clear and piercing sound that all the people of the western mountains could have heard it. The city erupts once more, and the clamor rises to an almost frantic volume. Everywhere, voices cry and exclaim.

"He's become a god! The gods have made him their own!"

"See how the divine powers shine upon him!"

"None can defy him!"

Beside Thehlýnin, the girl claps her hands to her ears, a shocked and unsettled gleam in her golden-brown eyes.

"Let's get away from here!" she yells to him, pointing through the mob to the stairs that lie somewhere beyond. He nods gratefully in reply, slipping gently between the shoulders and elbows of the crowd. And he lifts his head one last time as he goes, glancing toward the mighty steps of the House he once called home. Just one glance more—then the thickness of the air grips him. And for a terrible moment he is hardened in his place, standing helpless as the throng presses all around him. Helpless as the golden face—the awful, grinning face of the man who stands between the columns below—turns to catch him in its horrible stare, somehow finding him in the sea of faces that swarms the scene. And for an instant Thehlýnin is trapped, entirely unable to turn away from the fire that churns within those eyes—the fire that burns suddenly brighter at the sight of the son of Távihn. For an instant.

Then the moment ends as suddenly as it began, and young Thehlýnin is running southward through the wild streets of Tekéhldeth with all the energy of his soul, not caring to secure the hood that flies at his shoulders, until the noise of the city falls and fades like dying thunder behind him.

29

The trees are full of green and amber light when I come gliding down between them, too focused on my landing to notice the figure standing in the leaves only a wing's length away. I'm still folding in my feathers when a lean but sizable rodent flops lifelessly onto the grass at my feet. A fresh kill. I look up to find Ilith's bright-eyed smile waiting.

"Caught it with my own strength," she says. "Borrowed nothing." I recognize a kind of static in the way she smiles, in the way she crouches with her weight at her toes. The spark that comes with the wonderful thrill of running. I laugh, bouncing once with my wings still partly opened.

"And Ekyán?" I ask.

"At the river again."

He's there every morning, ever since the attack. He tells us his bones are thirsty, that the water soothes the aches. And we don't argue. Only three days, and he's already slinking through the trees again with nothing but a tattered tunic to cover his wounded side. The bleeding ended long before he woke that first morning. Now it looks as if weeks have passed—new skin smoothing over the torn places, old scabs and dried blood falling away. It's a miracle. Though none of us have said it aloud, we all know. Hitérian is a miracle.

Three days. It's been hardly any time at all since we learned the second form of hitérian. But already our people can be seen running and darting through the trees from the faintest hours of the morning until the deepest dark of the night. Running! Running free and wild, without borrowing strength, without tiring. Running the way I ran the day I met Ilith and Ekyán.

Running until their hearts throb and the wind sings in their lungs. We're meant to run. We can feel it in our blood. It seems like we were dying only yesterday. But we've escaped—evaded that creeping death that once ruled our waking lives and tormented our dreams. We're not dying anymore. We're *alive*. Wonderfully, hopelessly alive, and it's almost too marvelous for us to fully understand. We'll no longer need to hunt in groups. We'll no longer count our steps from one grove to the next, no longer struggle for hours to climb the trees at night. We can *run*.

* * *

The sun is hanging toward the west when I go out alone again, flying over the eastern hills, beyond the edge of the trees. We've caught more food in the past three days than we know how to carry. I have no reason to hunt. Today, I just want to fly. And out on the hills the wind is restless. The tall grass of the prairie is rippling—dancing and shimmering along curving, sliding lines. Whites and silver-greens, stirring and swaying endlessly together. I pass leisurely over the green sea, letting the wind whip and roll over my head, my back, my wingtips. I could go on for days.

The woods are only a blotchy line along the western horizon when I turn back at last in a wide, slow curve. It's surprising—surprising to find that I could travel so far in what seemed like so little time, hardly taking notice of the effort. I can scarcely imagine the lands I might see if I followed the free currents in the wind. If I went the way the sun goes—drifting over hills and mountains and open seas until even the edge of the world might reveal its hiding place. And if *all* my people were virit . . .

My thoughts fall out and drift away on the wind when I spot something shadowed on a distant hillcrest, only a short glide away. A dark, unmoving shape that rises from the green waves and interrupts the shining lines there. I shift my feathers and drop a little closer, trying to make sense of the outline. I see it plainly as I pass overhead. And my heart cringes. It's alive, and big. Another one of *them*.

It's sitting with its back bent slightly forward. But its face is tilted skyward. And there's something different about the look of its head. The usual blue or greenish wrap has vanished. I bank against the wind and turn to circle over the sight. It's one of them, no doubt. But this one has uncovered its face—and for the first time I see that the Creatures—that *Man*—has fur. Or something like fur, anyway. The strands are long and wispy, the color of dry sand. I see them stirring and blowing in messy clumps as I drift nearer. And the hair seems to cover only the top and back of the head, framing a pale and naked face. A strange face. The sight of it turns something over in the deep corners of my mind, and I can't withhold a soft gasp from leaking out between my teeth.

Have I forgotten something?

It's a feeling I can't understand—subtle at first, but it grows. I circle over the man several times more, until the sensation is roaring in my head, and suddenly I'm turning up my wings and fanning my tail for a landing, without any plan at all.

I land a little way downhill from the man and stare, unsure why I've come, wondering how quickly it could leap from its place and snatch me away. Wondering if I could lift off in time. It saw me. It *must* have. It'd be difficult to miss something so much larger than even the greatest of the eagles in the sky. But I can't be certain. Maybe the man is blind. It makes no motion to acknowledge me. I breathe out, ignoring the way the wind lifts and ruffles my feathers.

It's just as big as the others I've seen. The face and neck are naked. Completely naked. And the face is unlike any I've seen in my waking memory—long and slender, framed by a strong jawline and a bony chin. The ears are short and rounded, upright against the sides of the head, and the nose is narrow, protruding from the face a little farther than the noses I see every day. And the eyes . . . they're small—not such a dominating feature as they are in the faces of my people. But they're eyes just the same. And now they turn to capture me in their gaze. These are the eyes—this is the face—that was once hidden from me, the face that somehow pulls at the ancient threads of my memory. I *have* seen such faces before. In dreams. Mobs and mobs of them. This is the face of Man. A face that raises confusing images in my mind—images of the Citadel, and of the presence that lurks there. And the thought slips bitter coldness into my heart. But somehow, I'm not afraid.

"You found your wings." The man tips his chin toward me as he speaks. *He*, yes. He's a man. And he sounds . . .

"I . . . yes," I whisper, wondering how he'll hear my reply at all, beyond the roaring of the wind. But a murmur is all I can manage. "How . . . you knew that I would?"

He takes a moment to squint casually up into the sky, at the surrounding hills. The way he moves— the curve of his back, the way his hands hang loosely over his bended knees . . . have I seen it before?

"I saw that you would, when I set you free," he tells me at last.

I can only stare. The Creatures—Man—have always been something for us to fear. What makes this one any different? He smiles softly as I watch, shows me the wide palms of his bare hands. A gesture that I somehow recognize as a symbol of peace.

"Come, I won't harm you," he says. "You know that already."

Now I'm certain. It *is* him—the same man who spoke to me once before, that horrible night when I was captured. I find my feet and begin to shuffle slowly up the hill, full of mixed and unsettling ideas.

He let me go, I remind myself.

He watches silently as I approach, remaining open handed all the while. I reach the crest of the hill stepping sideways, coming to a stop just a few paces from his side. Just close enough to stretch my wing and touch him. If I dared.

"You *saw* it?" I find the courage to speak a little louder, but the words are still little more than a gasp. The man gives a subtle nod, and I watch his expression shift. The calm smile fades. Something softens the hard lines around his eyes, and his gaze becomes a stare—a stare unlike any I've felt. A stare that pricks my mind and sends an odd shudder along my nerves. I blink.

"What do you see now?" I ask him. His smile returns.

"Someone dear to you."

For a moment my voice chokes back somewhere deep in my throat. Could he mean . . . ?

"Thayl?" I whisper.

"He came to many of our camps, your friend. And he spoke our language. Some have heeded his warning and returned to the West."

What? *Thayl?* He *is* alive! Suddenly there are ten thousand ideas in my mind. And I'm not sure which one to chase first.

"H-how do you see it?" I feel so stiff. The man shifts his weight, leaning back on one long arm.

"It comes like a daydream, or a memory," he tells me. "They have a word for people like me. They call us *vilt'e*, dreamers." A daydream, a memory . . .

"There are others like you?"

He shrugs mildly. "I've heard that there are, somewhere."

"Where do you come from?"

"From the West, far away," he tells me. "As do the others. But my trade has often led me over the Black Mountains and into these lands."

"Trade?" I repeat.

He nods, and something like a simple look of contentment spreads across his bare, narrow face.

"A stone carver," he says. I smile too, and realize with subtle surprise that I'm beginning to feel strangely at ease here, standing beside one of the race of Man. The beings that killed Kehlvi.

"I knew I'd find you here, if I waited. I came to warn you," the man says. I look back to him.

"Warn?"

"A number of my people have decided that your kind has some sort of connection to the curse on this land. They take you to be a bad omen—a sign of the presence that stalks the ruined city."

"You've seen it too?" I almost feel my eyes watering at the renewed thought of it. Such blackness, such suffocating presence.

"It lingers near our camps, now and then. Not long ago it took possession of a man."

Took possession. The terrible scene of our struggle in the woods comes flashing back to me. The way the attacker leaped and clawed after Ilith—thrashed and swatted like a wild animal. The man looks at me from the corner of his eye.

"But you shouldn't fear it," he says. "All fallen spirits are ultimately subject to the command of the living, and can only take you if you allow."

Only if I allow. I blink the subtle moisture from my sight, stuck momentarily on the words that have come to my ears.

"It's not the dark presence you should fear, but the men. They plan to hunt you, in the coming months. I can't stop them," he tells me, "but at least I can warn you. I suggest continuing south. Quickly." And he glances to the north. "Maybe you can outrun the curse too."

"Curse? Is there a curse?" I ask, almost holding my breath. He glances back to me for a moment, saying nothing. And I begin to wonder if I shouldn't have asked.

"I'm not sure what to call it," he says at last. Then the man turns to face me directly, moving suddenly from his place to crouch immediately before my eyes, leaning in more closely than I could ever find comfortable. I can see the tiny golden hairs on his cheeks, the shallow sky-hues in his eyes and the long, pale lashes that frame them.

"My name is Kéthreo. I'm the only man who knows what you are." His words set my heart suddenly racing, and the questions erupt all at once in my mind. But there's no chance to speak. "I want to help your people escape this land. If you're lost, just say my name, and I will see it. I will come," he tells me.

Then he stands, and his height is dizzying. My nose is scarcely higher than his knees. I look up, unable to hide the astonishment on my face. He takes the blue wrap from his shoulder and throws it roughly around his head and neck, leaving it loose like a thin veil over half his face. And he begins to stride away to the north before I can let more than a faint gasp escape my mouth. But he takes only four massive steps before turning to face me one last time.

"I must return. Go south. I will come," he repeats. And then he's gone on his way. He's a wavering blotch on the northwestern horizon before I can think to move. And even then I can only turn in place, shuffle my wings—unable to stop the echoing of his words in my head.

"I'm the only man who knows what you are."

30

"Ilith, do you remember Man?"

I find her rinsing clothes at the edge of the river, not far upstream from Ekyán. They found a few new decent shawls and loose tunics the day we searched for rope. Ilith rises from a crouch and stares blankly back at me, a sopping gray shirt in her hands. I wonder if it's for Ekyán. He could use a new one.

"'Man,'" she murmurs. "It sounds . . it sounds..."

"Familiar," I finish the sentence for her. "Like something we once knew all about."

"Familiar, yes." She blinks, and I watch her thoughts come back from some faraway place. "What made you think of it?"

I step closer to the sandy bank.

"I've seen what Man is, Ilith. I remember now."

"What do you mean, you've 'seen'?"

"The monster that attacked Ekyán, it was of the race of Man. So were all the others."

"What? Those massive, beastly things? But how do you know?"

"Because he just told me, the one who set me free," I say.

"WHAT? Just now? Did it follow you back?"

I shake my head, raising a wing as if to muffle the sound of her surprise.

"And he told me something else," I continue. For some reason, I'm almost whispering. "We need to keep moving. They're coming after us."

Ilith's mouth turns to a straight line, and her voice falls to a low, level tone.

"All of them?"

"I'm not sure," I tell her. "But it means I'll need your help with something."

* * *

We tell the others when evening comes. It isn't rare for us to gather together at the edge of dusk, sharing the day's discoveries as we climb excitedly among the shaded arms of the trees. It's become a time for the sharing of fresh thoughts and ideas, for the counting of heads and assuring ourselves that all are still living, still running. I've wondered all afternoon how the rest of our brothers and sisters would react to the news. But when Ilith and I tell them of the men, I'm relieved to see the calm courage in their faces.

"We can face them now, even if they find us. We have speed in our steps like never before. And they can't fight against our hitérian," one boy boasts, letting his arms hang loosely over the edge of the bough where he lies.

"How do we know to trust the word of one Creature? Maybe he's part of a trap!" gasps another from above.

"He was sincere," I say, shaking my head. "I could feel it."

"Whether the man lied or not, it would still be best to avoid any confrontations. We've all agreed already to leave this land. Following his advice would only mean that we do it faster," Lotánehl adds, talking as he climbs to a branch across from ours. "And they've used armor against us before. Maybe we should divide our numbers, move southward separately."

"And travel in slightly different directions. That way we can't all be found at once. I like the idea," Ilith says, bobbing her head beside me.

"We can aim for the same destination, say—"

"What about the place where the river begins to flow straight into the east? There's a huge boulder there, with a shape like a perching bird. I've seen it, from the sky," I say. No one disagrees with the idea, and in moments we've made plans to divide into seven groups—six of three and one of four. We all agree to stay within a two day's journey of the river, whether on the east side or the west.

I turn to my two dearest friends in our company. Ekyán sits peeking down from several branches above.

"As long as we have our hands, I'm not afraid of the men," I tell them. "I need your help."

Ilith gives me a sideways glance. "What are you thinking?" she asks.

"The virít is too frail to defend anyone. I need my arms back." I look down at the long sweep of my flight feathers, trying to ignore the sting of regret in my chest. I've fallen in love with the sky.

"You mean . . . change back? Can it be done?" Ekyán works the joints in his fingers as he talks, probably hoping to soothe the aching there.

"I don't know yet, not for certain. But I think we should try," I say. Beside her brother's dangling foot, Ilith has folded her arms.

"I'm sure it can be done," she says. "We decided not long ago that the *ek'let'eh* was probably triggered by carefully placed hitérian. Maybe changing back is no different. We can search for it."

It's a bright night after the sun fades. Full of stars. High in the trees, we sit awake. Searching, testing. Ilith presses her hands along my spine the way she did for Ekyán, sending soft currents of hitérian through her palms—experimenting with the flow, the feel. There are places where the energy seems to shift and reverberate more powerfully, like spinning undercurrents in a river's flow. Some are located between the spine and the shoulder blades, and others somewhere along my lower back—but the greatest surge is elsewhere. Ilith finds it when she lays her palm over the back of my neck, letting her fingers follow up along the curve of my head. The wave of heat and static that rises beneath her hand pulls a soft gasp from my throat. And I can't suppress a twitch in response, when it comes.

"I think you found it," I rasp.

"You sure you want to try this?" I can feel her hand wavering, ready to lift away. I take a moment to breathe, to find the firmness in my bones.

"It'll be just fine," I tell her.

The second time, the surge of energy is almost consuming. Hot, but not painful. It sears like rolling flames along my bones, my veins—lighting every nerve, every muscle. It burns the way it burned ages ago, when I leaped between the columns of the Citadel—bursting and sparking over my spine. And when it fades at last, I can hardly keep the balance in my legs. I grip my claws into the skin of our branch, fanning my wings to stay upright. Ekyán reaches out to stop my tipping, and Ilith catches me from behind.

"I think it worked," I stammer. My head is buzzing. Ilith laughs.

"I hope so," she says, "or I just fried your insides on accident. Maybe you'll change into a lizard this time."

31

They sit in silence at first, wedged in a narrow place between two taverns at the southwestern edge of the city. For some reason, it was the first place he thought to run to. There's scarcely enough room to let out his legs. So he sits with his arms folded and his knees bent up to his chin. He looks up. The girl is less cramped, sitting near the opening of the alley with her gaze on the empty streets outside.

"I've seen him before, that man." He stares ahead, talks to the bricks that rest little more than an arm's length from his nose.

"When you came here before?" She almost whispers. He nods.

"I lived here. Nine years ago. I was fourteen." He's never told her. She brings her arms together to hug her knees before looking up.

"What do you think happened back there?" she murmurs.

"Something terrible," he says, and he finds himself shaking his head in disbelief. "Could you feel it? The thickness in the air when he appeared?"

"Like the weight of a nightmare," she says, staring back at him. And Thehlýnin can see the stiff line in her jaw as she talks, and in the curve of her neck. Fear made visible. He tips his head back against the cool bricks, ignoring the way the mortar pricks and pokes at his scalp. It's strange—ridiculous even, the idea that's crept into his mind. And he doesn't expect her to believe it. But at the very least she might listen. And he has waited for someone to listen. Waited for years.

"I heard old stories, in the West. The people there say the stories are kept from the beginning of the world. Ideas forgotten ages ago in the cities of East Ataran," he tells her, and he closes his eyes. "That man reminds me of the old tales."

"What sort of stories? You mean the legends of the kings?"

He shakes his head.

"Something even older," he says, and he strains to remember the words in his memories. "In the West they say there will be some in the world who are meant to stand apart from the rest. Like shepherds over the flock. They call them *Sasariane*, 'the judges'—people gifted with some kind of divine authority. They're said to stand between the people and the gods themselves."

The girl is silent at first—probably suspecting him to be a superstitious fool. And maybe she'd be right. Maybe he never should've mentioned—

"Representatives. Like the officers of the Voice?" Her reply breaks the slow sinking of his thoughts. Soft, unexpected. And he opens his eyes to find her still staring, waiting.

"Maybe," he says. "But I don't understand it— I never needed to. Only yesterday it was just some senseless legend, just a tale."

"So, what are you saying? Do you—you think what happened here is . . . ?" Her voice slides away, lost in the curious frown on her face. Thehlýnin rises partly and shuffles down the alley to sit beside her, letting his voice slip into a whisper without knowing why.

"Did you see it? The guardian at his side?"

"You mean his staff? It was floating in the air, like it weighed nothing at all."

"It's alive."

"*Alive?*" Her forehead wrinkles to give room to her gaping eyes.

"I heard about them in the West," he tells her. "The *k'rerehgen*—not staffs but living creatures, given to the Sasariane. Like some kind of guardian or servant for them."

"But how—what purpose does it all have?"

He shakes his head.

"I don't know. Maybe I've lost my mind. But it fits. The *k'rerehgen*, the power he carries, even the sashes on his golden robes. They mentioned it all, in the old stories. But I don't want to believe it. It's all too strange to believe."

"Doesn't seem like some heaven-sent messenger to me, that man," the girl murmurs. For some reason, she won't mention his name. But it doesn't bother Thehlýnin. He won't say it either.

"Maybe he isn't anymore," he replies. "Maybe he's taken his power and chosen to become something else. Something terrible."

For a moment, they both drift away in their own thoughts, and nothing but the subtle sounds of the outer lanes hang in the air between them. Beyond the tavern walls, a little crowd of birds hops and flitters by, scavenging for crumbs among the cobble—either unaware or unconcerned with the two figures hiding in the alley, entirely disconnected from the troubles of the city, the fears and the helplessness of the people. If only the son of Távihn could join them—rise up in the afternoon breeze and forget about the burdens of humanity. There was a time when he thought he could.

His friend shuffles her feet beside him.

"You said 'they,' when you mentioned the judges. Are there others?" she asks. It's a thought that hadn't occurred to him. A fact lost in the endless tumbling of ideas in his mind. It's true, the stories always mentioned . . .

"Two," he murmurs. "They say there are always two in the world, together. A man and a woman."

"Then where's the other?"

At first, Thehlýnin only blinks. The *other*. Is there another? Another shining, fiery countenance, another terrible gaze? Another merciless ruler? Could there be? The thought is puzzling, and when it comes to his ear he finds himself caught somewhere between a laugh and a cry. Maybe it's all ridiculous. Maybe the terror of past years has obscured his judgment, turned him into a superstitious, hysterical young man. Maybe the stories are stories, and nothing more. He makes a valiant effort to pull his mind away from the scene, to look at it all from some outside angle, but even as he tries, he can't ignore the growing stiffness in his lungs—and the sight of the horrible face from the Grand Way that seems to rise again and again in his mind's eye, burning an ever-deeper trench into his memory. And at last he's forced to recognize the awful reality of it all, the almost tangible details of the memories that weave there. It was *real*, what the people saw today.

"I don't know," he tells her at last, feeling lost. Maybe there's no more line between history and superstition, between real and unreal. Maybe silly stories are all they have left to explain what's happening in the Golden City. And he wonders what sort of stories they'll tell of Tekéhldeth, in ages to come. If there will be anything or anyone left to remember.

"East Ataran has always been our home," she says. "But we can't stay any longer. Father and I have been trying to convince the others in the western lanes for months. And I think they might finally agree." The girl pauses to place a gentle hand to his back. "You should come with us." The orange light of day is leaping off the pavement, painting a subtle glow onto her pale face and hiding the freckles there.

Leave Tekéhldeth behind, again? Somehow, it doesn't seem possible. But it must be.

''I can think of nothing better,'' he tells her.

32

Lately I sleep later than I ought to, but the others don't seem to mind. Especially not Ekyán, who long ago became too stiff to climb anywhere very quickly. Stiffness, aching—it's all happening the same way it did for me. He's changing. We didn't mean to trigger it, that night. We only wanted to heal his pain, his wound. But it's happening. I watch as he crawls awkwardly between the branches, working his way to the forest floor. Maybe he'll become a virít.

I'm not much better myself, this morning. But my own pains aren't bad—not like I remember. Fortunately, we've learned to use hitérian to soothe the aches. And I'm more than glad. I don't care to remember the discomfort that nearly paralyzed me the night Kéthreo found me.

I open my dark wings and shake the thick heaviness of sleep from my feathers. It's been a slow journey. We followed the river's south-winding path for three days, until its flow made an arch to the west. Then we kept to our southward course for another five. Now the river has curved back into our path, and we've slept two nights within the sound of its voice.

We continue southward along the bank of the river all morning, moving at a fraction of our usual speed. Ekyán's steps seem to grow more labored as we go, slowing to almost a crawl by late morning. It's still early in the afternoon when he stops entirely in his place, breathing deep, staring down to the leaves at his feet. I come down from a lazy glide and land near his side, careful not to excite the dirt in my path. The sun slides between the bodies of the trees and paints yellow stripes along the left side of his face, forcing his big eyes to squint. Ahead in the trees, Ilith pauses to look back.

"Is something wrong?" she asks. She waits for only a moment, then comes rushing to meet us when her brother doesn't respond. She puts a hand to his heart. "We should stop here," she says.

The change is coming closer. She holds him for what seems like hours, sending soft hitérian into his heart and shoulders, until he falls asleep. By nightfall, a thin shell has grown over his body and covered him entirely, like an eggshell not yet hardened. And I can't seem to stop marveling at the sight of it.

"There's still so much we don't understand— even in the nature of our own bodies," I murmur, staring over my shoulder at the pale cocoon that lies in place of Ekyán, beside the water. Ilith tends the tiny fire between us.

"We'll learn in time," she says.

We won't be going any further tonight. Or for many days to come. We have no way to carry Ekyán. If the process is anything like my first experience, he may be asleep for several weeks. And I'm not far behind him.

It's difficult to wake, when morning comes again, and by midday I'm too stiff to fly.

"How will you manage alone?" I ask Ilith as we sit by the river's edge. "We can't get into the trees this way."

She shakes her head. "Don't worry about me. I'm not scared of the dark or the beetles in the grass, remember? And anyway," she glances around at the water, the trees, the patches of sky up above. "This place has a good feeling about it. I think we'll be fine."

When the heaviness comes at last to my mind only two days later, I welcome it. I settle myself between the thick roots of a massive tree and try to focus on something beyond the aching in my bones. I close my eyes and remember the way the wind felt as I soared within it, the way my heart raced on the updrafts, the sweeping turns, the slow glides.

"I'll see you when I wake," I murmur, assuring myself just as much as Ilith. If she replies, I don't hear it.

33

They ring the bells from the four edges of the city. One by the south gate, one by the eastern hills. One by the north wall, one by the western lanes. Ringing in one voice, a low and heartless tone that swells and sways in the alleyways—leaping from the tower walls and pressing like a rolling, numbing tide into the people's hearts.

One toll. And all the people rise together. Two tolls. And all the inn and cottage doors are left open. Three tolls, and all the people fall in unison to their knees. All bow to adore their lord, their mighty king, who is only a little less than the gods themselves. He who has united the Ten Regions, laid down their borders and brought them in as one kingdom beneath his merciful hand—he who is the one true Directing Hand. He whose glory the people bend to worship, when the bells toll with each setting sun.

They say the great king rides up on the wind to the far edges of the world, descending where he will, watching where he will. They say his fiery splendor is often seen in the cliffs of the southern regions, lighting ablaze the red stones there, rivaling the last burning rays of dusk for glory and radiance. There he descends to commune with the earth, and with the gods. For he is near to their grandeur. And there are none that move without his gaze.

34

"We should have left long ago. We can't remain here." Her voice is so faint; Thehlýnin almost fails to hear it at all. He struggles to shift his left foot to a less cramped position, barely managing to avoid kicking his neighbor in the process. The old woman from across the lane. It's the fourth time this week that they've crawled down here, where there's only room for two or three people to huddle together with the dust and dirt and darkness. This time, it was the girl's sister who risked hiding in the garden shed outside. She was coming in from the outer field when the bells tolled. Their father is still working away in the eastern orchards, and their mother is somewhere in the city. Thehlýnin sighs. At least the cellar is dry. At least they *have* a cellar to hide themselves in—rather than being forced to bow down to the demon king with the blades of the royal guards at their backs.

How long must this go on? Two days have passed since the decree was sent out anew. A proclamation read atop every tower and sent to all the kingdom, calling for vengeance—justice upon the most wretched traitor who still lives to curse the lands of East Ataran.

Justice! Retribution!

All the city cries for the blood of the conspirator who slew the eighty-first Eviskýoneh, who dared to flee from the honorable hand of the then king-to-be. Find him! They must find him—for the blood of the traitor must be had. And if not his, then as much of the blood of the less-loyal citizens as it takes to pry him from his hiding place. The girl is right. They can't remain here.

"What path will you take?" he asks her.

"Almost straight west. Mother will go to send a message for Father, and we'll meet just beyond the southwestern docks." She looks up at him, but Thehlýnin can only guess her expression in the meager light. "You're coming with us, aren't you?" she questions.

He gives himself a grim smile. That was the plan, wasn't it? West. The very thought of returning west brings relief like a morning breeze to his mind. But there's something locking him to this cursed land, this haunting city. There's a twisting in his heart that can only grow—a kind of churning, festering weight that's grown too large to remain any longer. Something he needs to solve. Can the son of Távihn hide, while the people are slain at the north wall on his behalf? They say ten have been brought and bound already beyond the walls of the House. How long can they wait?

She's the only one who knows his name. And one of the four people in Tekéhldeth who might care if he vanished.

"Don't worry," he tells her. "I'll follow behind."

35

Everything's so hot, so wet, when I wake. Wet like a pond on a misty summer afternoon. There's a nasty clog in my throat, and a faint scent of blood in my nose. Like before, when I woke as an eagle. But I'm not a virít anymore. Not this time. I can feel it. I cough and hack and attempt to blink the haze from my eyes. But there's only soft light and blurring shades. Dull shapes and shadows. Nothing to see. I find myself relying entirely on touch.

Arms, hands, fingers! I can feel them all. I have *arms* again. And I'm so desperately thirsty.

I stretch out my arm against the film that encloses me, try to tear it with my sleepy fingers. It pulls apart like the thin husks on the fruit we used to find in the ruins. New air rushes in through the opening I make, clean and cool and full of scents. And sounds.

"Lorëu!"

I struggle to sit up and swipe away the remains of the soggy shell. I'm still bending the stiffness from my back when a blanket falls over my shoulders, and I find myself suddenly pulled into cradling arms. And a certain smell surrounds me—a scent like prairie grass, like a gust over the hills when the sun has only just begun to set. Something I thought I might never smell again. My heart chokes and halts in its place, and I lift my hands without thinking—reaching frantically up to touch the shoulders, neck, and face of the blurred and shaded figure that holds me, breath failing me.

"Is it—is it—" The words tangle and run together in my mouth. And my voice is so exhausted. I hear him laugh—a kind of gentle sob that sends a warm puff of breath over my reaching arm. But when he speaks, there's a smile in his voice.

"You're still brown," he says at last.

"Thayl!"

His arms are tight around me, squeezing out what little breath remains in my chest, but I don't mind. Water streaks in cold lines over my cheeks, splattering onto his neck and creating wet blotches on the blanket between us.

"You—you're here!" I gasp. "But I thought, I thought—"

"I'm here. And I'm sorry. I'm sorry I took this long—"

"How did you escape?" The world is beginning to look more solid in my eyes as we talk. I focus on the curve of his shoulder, and the dark bodies of the trees beyond. It must be late morning.

"I'm still not entirely sure of that myself," he tells me.

"Where did you go?" I sit up to look into his eyes. My vision is clearing more rapidly now, though I can hardly believe what I'm seeing. His face turns distant.

"To dark places," he says, and there's a flicker of dread in his eyes. But he keeps it calmly tethered behind the peaceful smirk I know so well. "I can tell you more when you've fully recovered."

I watch the reflections in his eyes, searching for words. Where do I begin? How can I possibly tell him of all that we've been through—all we've seen and discovered, escaped and survived?

"So much has happened, Thayl," I say. "I wish you could've seen it. We're not dying anymore—and I had wings!"

He laughs again.

"I *did* see it, from afar," he says. "You were like an eagle! I thought I had lost my mind! But it was real, and it was amazing." He reaches to secure the blanket that threatens to slip off my soggy shoulder. "I'm sorry you had to be alone, when you woke. I meant to return sooner to the place where I left you."

I blink.

"Left me?" I try to remember, and in a moment the night comes back to me—when I collapsed in the woods, trying to run from the camp of men. The night I was set free. I thought it was an illusion, when he came. I thought my mind had failed me. And until now, I'd forgotten all about it. "Then it wasn't a dream," I murmur.

"*Bálaye!* It worked!" I hear Ilith's voice ring out from somewhere nearby, and she comes leaping from between the trees, green eyes beaming. She lands beside us and makes no delay in looking me over—grabbing my left wrist and holding out my flimsy arm for inspection.

"So? How do you feel? Looks like arms and hands to me! Are you back to your old height? Have you tried to stand yet?"

She makes me laugh out loud.

"Not yet," I tell her, and I find my feet. With Thayl's support, I manage to rise with wobbly knees. Were my legs really this long, before I became an eagle? I look down at them. The fur is damp and matted— shining with an almost slimy gleam in places. And the faint scent of blood still lingers at my breath. I look up to my friends with a cringe. But Thayl only grins and shakes his head.

"We'll take you to the river," he says.

* * *

"Where's Ekyán?" I ask them as I sit curled by the fire, watching the wild embers dance in the midday light. We don't often use fire, these days. But it will help me dry off. We keep it small.

"He woke about eleven days ago," Ilith tells me, shaking the leaves from her shawl. "You should've seen it."

I glance at Thayl, hoping to find a hint in his face, but he's watching the fire. He sits with a tree-green sash draped loosely over one shoulder and tied at his side. I wonder where he managed to find it.

"Did he become a virít?" I wonder aloud.

A spark of excited light seems to rise and flicker suddenly in Ilith's eyes. "Something else," she tells me.

Something else?

"Something new?" I ask.

She nods. "Something meant for water. He left in the river that afternoon, wanting to see where it goes. He swims like the fish, now."

I hug my knees to my chest, beginning to feel dry at last, trying to make sense of the idea in my head. I stare into the fire. Something meant for water.

"First the eagle, now a fish," I mutter. "Where's the limit?"

"I've no idea," Ilith says. "But let's not try to find it just yet. I've seen enough changing to last me a while. It's a good thing your friend here showed up. I might've started talking to myself."

I laugh.

"You're all dried off. . . ." Thayl's voice trails off as he rises and slips away from the fire. Before I can question, he returns from behind the nearest towering tree and lays something over my shoulder—something the color of a midnight sky.

"My sash!" I leap to my feet. It's something I haven't seen since before my days as a virít. I wrap it the way we always do, over my shoulder and around my waist, finishing with a knot at my back. Atop the deep-violet tunic Ilith found for me, the color of my sash seems to glow. I feel like royalty. I look back to my friend.

"Thayl! How could I ever hope to thank you enough? Where did you find this?"

"I took it when I found you collapsed in the northern woods," he says. "Didn't think you'd need it while you slept inside a slimy shell."

I lay a hand to the dark weaves of the fabric at my side as he talks. There's moisture blurring my eyes, and I can't understand why. What is it about this color that pulls at the forgotten places of my heart? That brings Évrieth to my mind? Somehow, Thayl knows. He takes my hand and grips it tightly.

"Someday soon, the pieces will all come together," I whisper to him. "I can feel it."

* * *

We stamp out the fire and head southeast as soon as we fill our water satchels, talking as we move through the trees. It feels so wonderful to walk swiftly again. Thayl walks beside me, lifting his hand to draw a line from my head to his in the air between us.

"You *did* return to your original height, or something very near it. How do our bodies do it?" He shakes his head in wonder.

"It's all triggered with carefully placed hitérian. We're certain of at least that now," Ilith explains without turning, ducking beneath a low branch in her path. I follow her motion, then turn back to Thayl.

"It's taken us months to figure it out. Where you pushed me, in the Citadel—hitérian on both sides of the spine, between the shoulder blades. It's the spot that will change us to virít," I tell him. "And now we know that hitérian through a single palm to the back of the neck and base of the skull triggers a return to our original shape."

Thayl nods softly as he walks, and I can see the thoughts passing like shadows over his face.

"And what about the *virkepa*, the river creature Ekyán's become?" he asks. I smile at the name he's given the new form. *Virkepa*, "big fish." I can already sense that it's going to stick. Ahead, Ilith puts a pale hand to her hip as she walks, thinking. The afternoon sun seems to highlight her nearly white color. She almost glows.

"I sent energy through both hands that night. One laid along his lower spine and the other on his left side. I guess either placement could have triggered it. Or the combination of the two," she concludes.

"What do you think it all means, for . . . ?" I drift off midsentence.

"For what?" Ilith glances over her shoulder. I'm not sure how to frame my thought.

"For us? For who and what we are?" I ask. Ilith only shrugs.

"I'm not sure I'll ever make sense of that," she calls back. At the edge of my view, Thayl's gaze turns to follow me. But I'm suddenly too lost in my thoughts to respond. The image of a man's narrow face comes back to me. Sky-colored eyes and sandy hair—and words I once heard, the low voice that carried them. Words that weigh like great boulders on my heart.

"I'm the only man who knows what you are."

* * *

Evening finds us in a grove not far from the river's ongoing edge, in a place where the earth is beginning to rise and fall more sharply under our feet. There's little foliage between the massive pillars of the trees, and as we walk the wide, open spaces among them, I can't seem to shake the constant gasp of awe from my mouth. Here we've found the palace of the trees. A place where memories of the forests of long ago lie sleeping, twisted and folded into the stiffened bark of the ancients that remain here. It's a grove that's endured for generations. Standing at its heart, I feel as though I could reach out to grasp the thick layers of time that have whirled and settled in the air here—settled for years. And I wonder who may have tread these paths, in ages past. Tonight, it will be *our* camp.

I don't suppress my urge to explore. Ilith and Thayl are using the rope to secure our little food supply in the lower branches when I allow myself to wander alone to the east, where the forest floor climbs steadily skyward. I lean into the slope and press my way upward, grasping branches here and there for support until I come to the crest. And an idea floats gently into my mind.

"Just say my name."

The concept is strange—beyond strange. It sounds like something from some old, silly myth. How could it possibly work? But I shake my head and try to let go of the logic in my mind. Since the moment we discovered hitérian, the world hasn't ceased to prove its unpredictability, I remind myself. Didn't I just learn how to rise like an eagle on the wind? And what is it that happened with Ekyán? I don't know everything. In fact I know very little—I don't know who or even *what* I am. What authority could I possibly have to say what is and isn't possible? And now that the idea comes to my mind, I *need* to ask him.

I come to a solitary place in the trees and glance around. There's nothing but massive trees and a few bulky stones. It feels a little ridiculous. But it can't hurt to try.

"Kéth—"

I hear rustling to my left before I can finish pronouncing the name, and I turn to find a familiar, massive shape stalking toward me through the trees. A figure nearly twice my height with limbs as thick as those of a young tree. It's him. This time, I'm not a tiny virít. But his height still astounds me. As does the fact that he has just miraculously appeared with perfect timing. My eyes must be wide enough to fall from my head.

"Y-you came," I stammer, marveling silently at the subtle vibrations his steps send through the dirt. The man's face is almost entirely cloaked when he comes into full view, but I recognize the eyes.

"Of course," he replies, and he steps past me to bring himself down on the nearest stone. It's low to the ground, and he's forced to sit with his knees bent high in the air before him, but he doesn't seem bothered. He pulls the wrap from his face in one smooth motion, unhooks a latch at his side, and tips a great flask to his mouth.

"But it must have taken days!" I whisper. Kéthreo slides a hand through his sandy hair, sifting the loose waves there.

"Nine and a half, yes, from the southwestern ruins," he tells me. "But I saw you call me long ago. You've kept a good speed. The men are still searching out the southern edge of the ruins for your trail." Then he's just watching me, and in a moment of odd silence I find that I've been standing with my hands clasped anxiously over my heart. For some reason, being so near one of the race of Man is still somewhat unnerving to me. After a time, he leans forward to rest his arms across his knees.

"Now, what have you called me for?" he asks. I search for the words to frame my astonishment.

"Why do you bother coming all this way for us?" I blurt out, still marveling. "What could you possibly gain?"

"Gain?" He almost laughs. "Is the satisfaction of knowing that this people will live on to become a mighty nation once again not a great enough reward? What greater motivation would I need?"

"But . . . you've journeyed so far! N-nine days?"

The man smiles softly, nodding to himself.

"I had a dream, many months ago," he says, "and I saw that some of our men would go to the ruined East and eventually attempt to destroy what they would find there, deeming it evil—only because they wouldn't understand it. I couldn't let a handful of my countrymen extinguish the last remnants of an entire race. I'm only one person. But I had to try." His stare is firm, but soaking with a kind of warm light that somehow sets my heart at ease. He's telling the truth. I know it.

"Why haven't you feared us, as the others do?" I ask.

"Because I watched," he replies, bringing his pointed chin to rest over his intertwined fingers. "Since the night I first saw you in the central avenue of the ruins, and nearly every day since."

His words bring me momentarily back to the night of Kehlvi's death, when we glimpsed the hulking figure in the Avenue. That night, the monster didn't attack us—didn't even try to follow us. Now I understand why.

"I very quickly discovered that you were as far from demons as any man could consider himself to be," Kethreo adds.

Demons. I think of the night I was taken away—to the men who snatched us from our sleep within the sound of the waterfall—and to the possessed man who clawed and crawled after us the night Ekyán was injured. And they call *us* demons. I take a breath, try to think back to the question in my mind.

"I . . . I called for you because I have a question," I tell him. "You said that when you see things, they come like dreams, like memories."

He dips his head softly. "Yes."

"Do you see only things to come?"

"Most often, yes," he replies. I search his gaze, hoping to see the answers stirring somewhere in the shades there. *Things to come.*

"How . . . how do you know? Do they always become reality? How do you know it isn't something that happened long ago? Or something that will never happen?"

The man's expression shifts now, and the soft shades that trace his features become set in place. He's staring into my mind again.

"You've seen something. Many things. Haven't you?" he says.

"I have. Since the beginning."

"What have you seen?"

Where to begin?

"Strange things," I answer, fingering my sash as I try to remember. "Paved paths, wide and narrow, and faces—endless crowds of them. Faces like yours, not mine. And a man—a terrible, shining man." I hold up a dark palm in the space between us. "And my body is different, in the dreams. It's . . ." I look up to Kéthreo, and my words are suddenly forgotten. He's uncovered his left arm—rolled the pale sleeve until it clings in a wrinkled ring just beyond his elbow—and held it out for me to see. It's bare, with only a faint frosting of golden hairs to cover the soft-toned skin. *Naked*, the way my own arms have appeared in the dreams. What does it mean? How do I understand it? I step closer, unable to stop the sudden heaviness in my breath. It's like *my* arm, in the dreams, like . . . I almost reach out to touch him—but I stop myself, pausing just beyond his giant knee.

"The dreams . . . sometimes I worry they'll become real. But they have a strange feeling to them. Like I've seen it all before," I tell him.

"I think they're memories, Lorëu." His answer is so calm and controlled that I wonder if he's always known it. And it's an answer that sets my heart thrumming in its place. I look up at him now, feeling suddenly overwhelmed and out of air. *Memories?* But I'm not . . . was I . . . ?

"You said—you said you know what we are," I stutter.

"I do." An eternity passes then, between the man and me. A seemingly endless instant that grabs like sharp static at every bend in my mind—leaves me hanging breathless and helpless on the moment before me. Questions! Questions that beg for answers— questions that rise as a great tide in my heart, threatening to burst and destroy any peace in my soul. At last I find the breath to speak.

"Will you tell me?" I ask him. "Did you see it? What happened here? To us, to our land?" I try to hide the urgency in my voice, but it creeps out in a soft tremor at the edges of my words. Kéthreo looks down to the forest floor for a time before turning back to me.

"I knew this land, as it once was. We all did. My tradesmen and I came often over the mountains with fine stone for the bridges and towers of the East. I was near the border when the merchants came fleeing west, bringing strange and terrifying tales. We've come from the West in hopes of understanding what became of the great people of the East," he says. "But unfortunately, far too many of us aren't willing to truly understand."

"The people of the East," I repeat. "What were we like? What were we called?"

He only shakes his head.

"Revisit your memories. I think you already know." And he unrolls his sleeve, smoothing it back into place. "I wanted to ask you and tell you so much more, when I first found you. But it would have been too much for you then, too confusing. These are answers I can't give you now, only because it's not my place. But the time is near when you will find them. I know you will. There are some truths you must reach on your own. And when that time comes, you will understand why," he tells me, and he rises to his feet. I remain dumbfounded before him, almost teetering, his words racing and whirling like stray leaves in the winds of my mind. The questions are beginning to drown me inside, and I no longer have the power to ask them. But then Kéthreo kneels down again to speak at my level. And his wide hand is gentle on my head.

"You already know who you are, Lorëu. Memories are never truly lost. They are your own. No one else can remember them for you. But you and your people can help each other. You can search for them together."

I nod in reply, fighting the tears that are welling up at the edge of my sight. I believe him.

36

She appears like the dawn on the southeastern hills. Stands with radiant robes trailing—with the glow of the morning in her countenance, the light of the stars in her eyes—and the rays of the rising sun pour like ribbons from her shoulders. She comes like an angel of the sun, a goddess in the wind, when she descends upon the hills. She comes with sorrow, to the great City of Glimmering Lights. And the stars weep beside her.

The people gather in awe-stricken throngs to see her. They gather where she descends at the south gate that evening—crowding the Grand Way and flooding the avenues in every direction. All come to see the Angel walking north to the heart of the city. And their faces shine like the midday sky, in her presence. A goddess! Come with hope, come to save. Come to join or oppose, raise up or destroy.

There are some who flee in terror from the Angel of light—flee to the great marble steps of the House of Voices for refuge. And high above their heads, upon the southern balcony of the House, their mighty king stands with hot dread in his eyes—stands with trembling hands gripping the marble handrail before him. His fiery gaze is locked far down the long neck of the Grand Way, on the south gate—where the people part like colorful waves in the Angel's path. She walks with slow strides long into the evening light, and when she comes at last to the steps of the House, the stars and moons have risen to their full brilliance in the dark face of the sky. But the light of the goddess surpasses even the glow of all the great torches in their golden dishes at the heart of the city. And she and the king become solid in their places. She, at the steps of the House, and he, standing frozen at the balcony's edge.

They stand unmoving, long into the night. Gaze for gaze—neither one bending to the other's glory. But there is living fire in the air between them. A burning that drives the people away. Some remain looking on for hours, watching until they become too weary and amazed to remain any longer. The sea of faces drips steadily away until the very deepest hour of the night, when there is only one figure standing at the steps of the House. And when she speaks at last, there are none near and awake enough to hear her words.

"Three days," she murmurs, and the night wind wicks up the sound, carrying it high against the tower walls. "I give you three days, my brother."

37

He walks with his head uncovered. Walks in the open darkness from the outer lanes and well into the eighth avenue without spotting any sign of life or movement in the maze of thick doors and boarded windows that leads to the center of the city. The people of Tekéhldeth are hiding from the night. A long night. There are no golden-sashed soldiers stalking the midnight streets, as there have been for years. Tonight something is changing. Something tremendous. And it's expanding in the breath of the city. Heavy, and almost tangible—like the thickness in the air that comes and blankets the hills before the rain. And Thehlýnin can feel it in his lungs.

He can see the glow of her countenance streaming over the brick and cobble of the alleys ahead long before the Grand Way comes into view. And when he sees her at last, the white light of her presence closes in like pure and brilliant mist all around him. A kind of infinite whiteness unlike any he has ever seen. Or ever imagined.

She has stood unmoving for a night and a day in the square before the House, her undying gaze directed to the marble balcony high overhead. An empty balcony. Now the second evening falls, and for the first time in nine years the son of Távihn finds himself standing entirely exposed at the heart of Tekéhldeth, in the deepest hour of the night. But this time, he isn't running. Perhaps it will be the greatest mistake of his life—coming here, to the doorstep of the demon who slew his father, only to talk with the woman they call a goddess. But somehow, he needed to. And for some reason beyond Thehlýnin's power to explain to himself, he is calm.

The Angel's hair is red, and it hangs in long scarlet waves over her magnificent robes. A deep and living color—like the wildflowers that spread their blooms along the city walls, fighting for brightness against the dust and pale mortar there. He only watches her at first, forgetting the tears and darkness and terror of the memories that scar this place. Forgetting any plan that may have formed in his mind.

Beside the shining woman floats the slender figure of her guardian—a limbless, almost featureless creature. A shape like the tall staffs of the priests in the West. But living. A silvery orb hangs near its top, suspended weightlessly between the two curved, thin points that frame the open-crescent shape of its head. The staff drifts soundlessly in the night air, seemingly detached from the forces of nature that bind and govern the reality surrounding it. When Thehlýnin speaks at last, he is near enough to watch the light swim and play like fluid glass in the guardian's single, shifting eye.

"Are you a goddess?" The echoes of his voice are swallowed up in the still air, falling wingless to the paved ground. But she still hears.

"I am Faliéhl, her servant," she murmurs. "As my brother ought to have been." Thehlýnin exhales and discovers that he hasn't breathed from the moment he entered the Way.

"Have you come to end what's happening here?" he asks her.

"I come with the hope of a better future for this people," she says, and the light plays in pearly lines over the scarlet waves that frame her face. Thehlýnin glances to the wide balcony overhead. A place where he once stood—in the memories of some other reality.

"Can you stop him?"

"I must, for this land to heal," she says, and suddenly her voice seems to come from far away. Many lands away, *lifetimes* away. And why is there rain on his face? He could raise his sleeve, could wipe it away, but he doesn't.

"Can it ever be healed?" he whispers, wondering how the sound could ever cross the great chasm between them. But when she turns her gaze to him, the gleam of her eyes sparks sudden wonder in Thehlýnin's heart.

"Yes," she tells him, and though soft, her words seem to carve into the cobble at their feet, into the weary stones of the towers and archways that surround them—and into the thick steps and pillars of the House. "All wounds can be healed. But it means we must be willing to change."

All wounds. It's true. And the truth has a way of opening him up inside, of tearing off the shutters on his heart and surging life into his veins—sending a wild gust of summer wind to sweep away the years of dust and soot and ash that have gathered there. Offering to revive the hopes that lie broken there. All wounds. He can feel it now—something new and precious in his heart, where nothing was before. A seed, an ember. A faint yet glorious glimmer in the shadows. And the broken boy clings to it with all his might, suddenly more alive than he has ever been, more awake in his soul than he ever knew was possible. Suddenly, there's a world of hopes and dreams and possibilities reborn before his eyes. And there's so much to live for.

All wounds. But we must be willing to change.

38

These southern lands have snatched my breath away from the day we first stepped within their borders. It's still early in the afternoon when we come to a place where the ancient columns of the forest give way to patches of open sky, and the tides of the earth begin to rise and jut up as jagged walls and towers all around us. The colors in the stones are aflame—crimsons and scarlets as thick and vibrant as Ilith's red sash, and they seem to dance against the living greens of the trees. I've never seen stones and earth so red. It's a sort of color that sets explosions in my eyes. As we climb and shuffle along, I often find myself blinking and shaking the glare of it out of my head. Above, the clouds have gathered themselves up into great towering mountains of billowing white, and the afternoon sun lights little sunsets in the broad leaves, making them glow with orange and green-yellow hues against the blue face of the sky.

We're moving down into the canyons now, learning to search for solid foot and handholds in the rocks as we go. I glance to my right as I climb over a nearly shoulder-high boulder and find Thayl watching something high in the parting canopy. Here, his dark color seems so sharp and sudden against the red stones. I can't withhold the little sigh that slips out from my chest at the sight of him. A breath of relief. He's still here. It's like a strange and wonderful dream, to have my friend beside me again.

Ahead, Ilith pulls herself onto a slanted rock to the side of our path and stands atop to glimpse the land beyond, lifting a hand to shield her eyes from the sun. I pause below with my head nearly level with her ankles. She's been oddly silent since we reached the canyon.

"What do you see?" I call up to her, surprised at the strength of the wind that comes gusting between the cliffs. It folds around Ilith where she stands, making her gray tunic whip and thrash against her slender knees. She lowers her hand.

"The river," she says, "flowing southeastward from the canyons ahead." She remains at her post for a moment longer before turning to slink down beside me. And there's a little frown at her mouth. "It's strange," she mumbles.

"What's strange?" I talk as I fumble to loosen the tie on my water satchel. Her delay makes me look up. And the red dust swirls in a fraying cloud before her white face.

"That the river appeared exactly as I expected it would," she says. "The way it always has, in the dreams I've had." I stare at her, waiting for more, but she only shakes her head and turns back to our path. If she hears me calling after her, she's too caught in her thoughts to respond. I *must* ask her.

We choose a crooked, strong-rooted tree for our evening roost. The sun begins to fade behind the cliffs and send yellow ribbons weaving through the branches as we climb. The tree is a brave one, daring to rise up along a narrow shelf in an east-facing cliff, where the rocks tip and slope sharply downward to the valleys below. We ascend slowly, leaving our rope raveled until we're ready to tie a securing line. Although no one says it aloud, we've all become fond of passing the night in places few other creatures would think to visit. Places where long arms aren't likely to reach in the dark. Thayl climbs to a massive bough just beyond Ilith's, and I crawl up beside him, looping the rope around one final branch and passing the end to him in the process. He ties it loosely to his wrist. We've never fallen, but we don't like to ignore the possibility.

Our tree has a wonderful view of the cliffs, as evening settles in. I sit with my back to the ragged bark and stare out at the night stars for a time, watching the way the clouds thin and wisp away, revealing the yawning, black-violet face of the night beyond. The stars beam like bits of silver scattered over a velvet sea—as if some ancient moon was shattered, and its sparkling remains lie strewn across the horizons. Maybe the view is too marvelous. None of us seem able to sleep. To my left, on the bough only slightly lower than ours, Ilith stirs. When I look, the stars have lit little lights in her eyes.

"I know this land. I've never come here, from the time Ekyán and I woke up in the hills up north. But somehow I've seen it before," she mutters softly. I turn to see her better, leaning into the tree's rough neck.

"In dreams?" I ask. She nods.

"Dreams. Except they often come when—"

"When you're awake?" I whisper the end of the sentence for her, and for a moment she only turns to stare back at me, maybe feeling the same sort of churning in her heart that's just begun in mine.

"Yes," she says.

You can find them together.

She's had them too. Maybe the answers are nearer now.

"Do you ever see yourself, in the dreams?" I ask. Ilith makes a little wrinkle in her chin as she thinks.

"I don't think so," she says. "What do you mean?" I sigh. To my right, Thayl has sat forward. He leans near my shoulder, listening.

"I've had dreams too. But not of *this* land," I explain.

"What've you seen?" I can hear the shift in her voice. The higher, smoother tone that always gives away her genuine interest in things. And her mother-like concern.

"Wide and narrow streets," I describe, "and crowds of people. But they aren't our people. People like . . . like . . ."

"Like Man?" Thayl's soft words finish where mine fall away. I turn to meet his gaze.

"Like Man," I echo, and for a moment, my thoughts pause in their place. "Thayl, do the dreams come to you too?" He stares back, and despite the darkness I can almost see it again—the subtle dread that flashed behind his eyes when I woke to find him at my side.

"I was trapped in the Citadel for ages," he tells us. "Hours, or days—I'm not certain how long it was. I haven't told you. When I escaped, it was only because I saw a path in a dream. A path that led beneath the marble halls to an outer court. The dark presence couldn't seem to find where I went until I was already out. I saw things in my mind, while I was there. And many times since. Like you have."

I sit up, feeling a flutter in my chest.

"So that's how you escaped," I murmur. "Have you . . . have you seen them too, in your dreams? Men?" I ask Thayl. He gives only a slow nod in response, and my heart plunges. Then it must mean . . . no. I draw circles around the idea in my mind, secretly searching for some way to avoid the conclusion my heart is already reaching. There must be another answer.

"I've seen him again," I start, "the man who freed me from the others. And when I told him about—"

"You *what?* Is he following us again?" Ilith nearly spits as she sits sharply forward, hairs on end. The rope at her elbow leaps with the motion and sends a gentle tug through the long coil.

"Don't worry!" I assure her. "He's trying to help us. He came back because I had a question. I wanted to ask if he knew what happened to our people. I wanted to ask if he knew what we are."

Thayl's eyes turn to almost perfect black circles. "Does he know?"

"He said he does. But he wouldn't tell me," I tell the distant cliffs, then turn back to Thayl. "And he once said that he saw you, Thayl. He said you could speak their language." I had forgotten to ask. Ilith nods, already calmed back to her usual self.

"Thayl told me a bit about that, while you were still sleeping," she confirms.

"It's true," he says, looking idly down through the branches, to the sleeping stones below. He brings a dark knee to his chest to rest his arm over it. "I can't remember the details, but I must've lived among them once. I found one of their camps after I escaped the Citadel, and discovered that I could understand their speech. But I can't entirely explain why. Not yet."

One of their camps? I breathe, trying to imagine purposefully walking into a camp of men. The idea makes my stomach twist. And it brings a cluster of memories to my mind—thick smells; low, rumbling voices; the cruel pinch of knotted cords at my wrists. I shudder.

"Did they try to hurt you? He said you warned them," I say.

"I told them to leave the ruins. That something dark is dwelling there. Some listened, but most were too shocked to listen. They seemed to think I was some kind of demon. They're determined to chase out the evil that's come to the land. But it's a hopeless effort." He shakes his head.

Evil. I remember the image of a man that appeared at the Avenue—the awful weight of its presence, the way it stood with arms raised triumphantly to the sky. The ruins of the Old City were always a strange place. But now they're something darker in my mind. A terrible place. A *cursed* place. Kéthreo's words rise again in my mind as I ponder, and the idea that I've fought to suppress returns to my heart—threatens to bubble out of my throat. I should tell them, but I . . .

"There's something else." My voice somehow creeps out on its own before my thoughts can finish, and I'm surprised to hear the words at my mouth. "I . . . I told the man about the dreams I have, and he says . . . he says the dreams may not be dreams at all. He thinks they're . . ."

"Thinks they're what?" Ilith tips her head in an attempt to fit into my downward stare.

"Memories."

The word is heavy on my breath. But it's a weight that feels right. We all sit motionless for a time, measuring the idea in our minds, turning it around again and again. And for the first time since the evening fell, I can hear the soft sliding of the wind as it weaves along the canyon walls. Ilith is the first to speak again, and when she does, her words are slow. Level voiced.

"Loröu, what do you mean, about seeing ourselves in the dreams? What've you seen?" She almost whispers. I open my hand in my lap and stare at the way my fingers bend, watching the soft angles in the joints there.

"I've seen . . . my arms and legs," I describe. "But they don't look the same. And if they're memories, I think . . . I think we were . . ."

Now the answer is throbbing in my throat. I know it—with all my aching heart, I know it. But for some reason, the word can't survive past my teeth. I can't say it. Not yet. For some reason, the answer makes me tremble inside. And the truth of it awakens a terrible sense of loss in my soul. The kind of burden that's dwelt within me since the morning my sister died.

A mild touch at my shoulder pulls me from my thoughts. Thayl's hand.

"Lorëu, months ago, when I found you standing out on a hill, you were listening to the wind there. You told me you had a strange feeling, like you were on the edge of a memory," he says.

"And you told me to keep listening," I reply. Why am I shaking so terribly inside? "Sometimes it scares me, what I see."

Thayl takes my hand now, enclosing it in his own.

"Don't be afraid," he urges, and the light of the stars behind casts a silvery outline over his black fur. "This is what we've been searching for. The man is right, Lorëu. We're beginning to remember who we are." He knows. I can see it in his eyes, can feel it in the grip of his hand. He knows what we were. And I know it too. But I can't say it yet. All this time, answers have ridden at the edges of our minds, flitting in the corners of our dreams, waiting to be pieced together. But we were too distracted with survival to take notice. Until recently, all our energy was exhausted on finding ways to survive, to convince our bodies to live on. Until recently, we were dying. But we're alive now. Perhaps the dreams have come to us all. And what will we find, in the scenes that remain there?

I lie awake for ages, after we talk. And when I dream at last, I dream of long, darkened corridors. Halls that seem to unfold endlessly before my feet, full of columns and tall, arching ceilings. Full of shadows, full of stone—cold, smoothed stone that catches and magnifies every sound. I dream of running there. Running awkwardly to muffle the clap of my sandals on the polished stone, following the blurred, shaded figure of someone in the path ahead. Someone with dark hair and eyes the color of the night sky. Sad eyes. Someone I know. I follow him for ages in the darkness there, wondering where he's fleeing to, wondering why he would ever choose to come here. And feeling afraid— so horribly afraid that I won't be able to stop him, afraid of the swelling in my heart that tells me something terrible looms beyond the next threshold. A premonition that tells me we can never go back. Not anymore—

I gasp, straining to see past the weariness in my eyes. *A dream, a dream. . . nothing more,* I try to tell myself, try to tunnel an escape with the words in my mind. But even as my thoughts race I'm hopeless to dispel the knowledge that sits like a rock in my heart. It builds and solidifies inside, rising until it rings aloud in my head. The knowledge that I wasn't sleeping, just now. And it wasn't a dream. It was a memory.

39

The sound of the river plays a wonderful rhythm through the valley, when we find it the following morning. A sound I've missed. It flows less swiftly here, but still fast enough to slap and spray against the mossy boulders that rise up occasionally from its depths. We spent the morning hunting for rodents. It was only a short journey down the first canyon wall to the water's edge. Now, as we bend to rinse our fingers and refill our satchels, the white gleam of morning is only beginning to fade along the treetops.

I stand and look southward, following the river's shining body until it curves out of sight. Ilith paces along the bank with her hands at her hips, staring intently at the woods that rise along the opposite shore. Thayl's the one who spots the motion in the water—an odd heave and ripple near the center of the river.

"What's that?" he wonders aloud, rising to his feet for a better view. I turn to watch with him. A fish? The ripple crosses to our shore. Then before I can think to move, Ilith has darted along the bank and splashed into the water. And when a wet figure rises suddenly from beneath the surface, she crouches down to throw her arms around his neck.

"You're back!" she squeals. The river begins to lap at her sides, turning her tunic from gray to black. I feel my mouth falling open.

"Ekyán!" I gasp, but for a time I'm too astonished to do much else. Thayl laughs. With Ilith's help, the wet boy pulls himself partly onto the sandbank, where the water flows just deep enough to lay slick, shining sleeves across his forearms. He lies on his stomach there, propped up on scrawny elbows. From the waist up, he looks basically the same. Aside from the thin webbing between his strangely elongated fingers.

"So tiring to swim upstream," he pants.

"How far did you go? Did you find the others?" Ilith always talks so quickly when she's thrilled. Her brother nods.

"Far," he says. "The river meets the sea, not far beyond the canyons."

"The sea! We're that close?" I marvel. How had I not seen it from the sky? Ekyán nods again, and the water falls like rain from the tips of his ears. At the river's edge, I squat down to see him better. His eyes seem glassier than before. Or maybe it's just the morning light.

"Found Lotánehl's group. They say to cross over," he says. He blinks, and I see the subtle sliding of clear films across his eyes. There *is* something different there.

Ilith glances westward over the river before turning back to him.

"Cross the river? Why?"

"They came through the canyon way, a few weeks ago. They said there was something strange on the east side."

Thayl appears at my side.

"What do you mean?" he asks. Ekyán tips sideways to shake the water from his head while he talks.

"Some kind of creature. Not a man. They thought you might miss it if you continued south on the west side of the river," he tells us.

Thayl and I exchange glances. Ilith only bites her lip.

"Then let's cross," Thayl says. "Couldn't hurt." I gladly agree.

The sandbars make crossing easier here than at other parts of the river. Toward the center of the flow, where the water is deepest, Ekyán swims at our downstream side, preventing the river from carrying our little bodies away. And I'm grateful. I'm a sloppy swimmer.

"Do you breathe underwater now?" I ask him as I flounder against the current. My chin is scarcely above the waves. He shakes his head, showing me his old grin. The bashful smile that Ilith loves to tease out of him.

"Just hold my breath," he says. He must hold it for a long time.

We only take a few moments to cross and clamber onto the western bank, shaking the river from our fur. I find a rock to stand on and grab my tunic in fistfuls to wring out the water—and can't help but laugh aloud when Thayl shivers like an animal, making the dark fur stand up in pointy clumps all over his body. But Ilith remains kneeling by the water.

"Ekyán, do you remember this land?" she asks, and I can see the answer in the wonder that floods the boy's face. He nods.

"I found a place south of here, by the shore of a stream that goes off west," he says, reaching to tug on his sister's soaked clothes. "You need to see." Ilith brings a hand to his shoulder.

"What kind of place?" she asks. There's a tremor in her voice. From where I stand, I can see a gentle crease appear in Ekyán's sand-colored forehead.

"A place we used to know," he says. Their home. Somehow, I can see it in his face. And the memory of the ruined cottage at the outer edge of the western ruins flashes softly over my mind. There's a silent moment between us all, and the rushing voice of the river becomes suddenly more obvious to my ears. Ilith turns to look at me with an urgency in her eyes that I haven't seen since the night Ekyán was injured—outlined by thin redness that seems to highlight itself against her whitish face. This is something they need to do. It's a place few of us have been fortunate enough to find. The place where our memories began. Thayl and I will be fine on our own.

"You should go," I tell her. "We'll find you at the meeting point, if not sooner along the river's path." I look to Thayl. He nods softly in agreement. Ilith sighs and returns to her feet—leaving little tracks in the sand behind her as she comes to me. Wetness somehow makes the leaf-green glow in her eyes more lively than usual. And her palm feels chilled on my cheek.

"Be careful," she says.

* * *

We untie our sashes and hang them in the trees to dry, after Ilith and Ekyán have disappeared to the south. They're too thick and long to be carried wet. I pull at the shoulders of my tunic, hoping to help the wind do its job. Wet clothes and wet fur always make such a wonderfully soppy combination. Thayl climbs the nearest branches and peers toward the southeast.

"Well, at least there are more trees on this side," I call up to him. "Probably more things to eat, too." He's high in the leaves, but I can still see the edge of his smirk from the ground.

"If that mysterious creature they saw doesn't eat us first," he replies.

We walk all afternoon and well into the evening. Night creeps into the canyon with the softness and subtlety of a predator at the hunt, sending its dark tendrils between the rocks, the trees, the bushes. I watch the shadows grow steadily longer in the path before us, and find myself idly wondering how Ekyán sleeps, as a fish. And whether Ilith will be able to climb high enough into the trees on her own. We should stop soon ourselves.

"Where do you think we should go when we reach the sea?" Thayl's question pulls me out of my thoughts. I tip my head to one side, thinking back.

"That reminds me of an idea I had," I say. "How far do you think we can fly, as virít? I never felt tired, soaring up in the wind."

Thayl looks to me, his ears shifting slightly backward as he thinks.

"I don't know. I guess as long as there's wind to keep us aloft," he says.

"Wind," I murmur, looking back to our path. "I usually depended on the big updrafts that come from the ground. They helped me climb high with almost no effort at all."

Thayl swats a nightfly away from his face.

"What are you planning? To fly over the sea?" he asks.

"I'm not sure if the updrafts exist over water. But maybe there's still a way." I try to imagine my wings again, try to envision how the air might flow over the ocean waves. But I've never seen the waves. Imagining will help me little. Maybe we could swim instead.

"Do you think there's land on the other side?" I ask. Until this moment, it never occurred to me that the sea may be large—impossibly large. Maybe it would be foolish to attempt to cross it.

"I think there is," Thayl says, and the confidence in his voice almost surprises me. "And besides, where else can we go? The men rule the west and north, and the darkness of the Old City seems to spread in every other direction." I sigh. It's true. Where could we go? Is the southern shore far enough to escape whatever curse has come to our land? Far enough to rebuild our people, our nation? I look up. Somehow without my noticing, the sky has become entirely black.

"I think we should stop for the night," I say. "It's already da—"

I don't finish my words before Thayl stops abruptly in his steps, gripping my arm. I stop awkwardly a half pace ahead of him. Looking onward, I see nothing but the shadows at first. The night is moving swiftly in, stifling the last of the evening's light from among the trees. But I look again. And then I've shuffled back to Thayl's side, suddenly unable to stop clinging to his clothes.

The shape sits hunched over in a space between the rocks, directly ahead. A rough, rigid shape with a hulking, uneven outline. The head must be sitting low, sunken somewhere out of sight in the shadow of its slumping body.

"What is it?" I whisper.

"I'm not sure," Thayl breathes back, and his arm is tight across my shoulders.

"Not—not a man," I say.

"Maybe an animal. Don't be afraid. Remember hitérian."

My mind races in a frozen body. Where can we run? Where's the nearest tree to climb? Can it climb trees? Why did we wait so late to stop for the night? Ahead, the shape remains motionless.

"Maybe we can back away, slowly. There's a tree not far, to our right," Thayl whispers. I do my best to give an audible reply above the throbbing of my heart in my ears. We begin a slow, backward shuffle, doing our best to avoid rustling too many pebbles at our feet.

Breathe. We're going to be fine. Just an animal, just an animal.

I try to talk myself into security, convince myself that there's nothing to fear. But I'm all the while helpless to pull my gaze from the shape that sits between the rocks. And my peace fails me entirely when a voice comes unexpectedly to my ear. Not Thayl's voice. Not any voice I've known in my waking memory. A whisper almost too thin to be heard, hanging in the air between us.

"This is my realm."

The voice startles us horribly. We both jerk impulsively backward and apart from each other, turning frantically around in search of the owner of the voice. But there's no one. And the space between the rocks ahead is suddenly empty. It comes at Thayl first— a dark, long-limbed and lopsided shape that attempts to wrangle him to the ground. I leap into the struggle and find one of the monster's long arms, ready to pull all the strength I find there—but there's nothing. No strength, no flowing energy. No *muscle*.

"Wha—?" I stammer in shock. The creature jerks free, and I resort to pathetic clawing and hitting, battling for another grasp. Thayl gives a valiant fight, pushing the beast away again and again. But it keeps coming. I take hold of its leg and jerk the bulbous foot in an unnatural angle, hoping to hear some kind of snap, or at least feel the twist of skin and tendon. But the foot slides like wet sand under my grip. What *is* this thing?

We become desperate, wild animals, swatting and tearing at the beast wherever we can. At last we manage to catch hold of the arm that locks around Thayl's neck and jerk it down together—it bursts and collapses against my knee, melting away into a fountain of dirt and sand that showers over my leg.

"Made of dirt!" Thayl exclaims, breathless—surprise and confusion swirling together in his voice. The beast tips backward. And for an instant, we're both free. We seize the open moment to turn and bolt westward through the trees, leaping over stones and ducking under branches as we go. How fast can it run? My heart is nearly leaping from my chest. I follow closely beside Thayl, trying desperately to make sense of it. How can this possibly be? It's something unreal, something far worse than men with wooden armor. How can such a thing live? Made of dirt! No bone, no muscle, no energy to steal. No use for hitérian. And without hitérian, what strength do we have? Our arms are little more than furry twigs at our sides. Without hitérian, we're *powerless.*

We only run for a short sprint before I see it again. And this time, there's no fight. It appears so suddenly at the edge of my vision—there's no time to dodge, no time to flinch or scream. A long arm catches me across the middle, knocking the breath from my lungs before I can react. Thayl turns, hand outstretched toward me, and for a fleeting fraction of an instant, I can see his eyes widening. Then my feet are swept from the ground, and the trees are whirring backward all around me. I claw hopelessly at the shape that pins me, all the while struggling to lift my head against the sharp jolting of the monster's run. But its body has turned rigid. Solidified, from mud to stone. *Stone.* I'm helpless. And so the monster carries me away like a fresh kill, dashing eastward over the night land. Or maybe southward, or northward. I have no way to know now. The world becomes a blur of dark hues rushing by—blacks and grays and shaded blues.

There's a part of me, floating somewhere at the surface of my heart, that gave up hope the moment the monster snatched me. A part of me that welcomed the impending end of the life I know. After all, how could I ever hope to break free from stone?

But I don't listen to it.

We've done hard things before, my people and I. We've had impossible struggles. And we overcame. And there's another part of me, woven somewhere in the fabric of my nature, that somehow knows, in some inexplicable way, that everything is going to be alright. That everything is going to be *wonderful*. Like the subtle chill in the night air that always whispers the promise of a new morning, or the fierce and defiant blueness of the sky when it peers out from between the graying clouds of a blustery day. And it's a knowledge I can't deny, despite the apparent hopelessness of my ordeal. Despite my complete inability to imagine my escape, or the fact that I can't seem to stop the terrible trembling in my bones.

We overcame before, when life's circumstances pressed and pushed us until survival was the only option. Until it forced us to turn to strength we never knew we had. Never *imagined* ourselves to have. We've overcome before. And now, we'll overcome again.

40

The sun has hidden its face on the day Thehlýnin Dredékoldn enters for the last time into the House of Voices. He walks entirely unnoticed among the people of the city, who wander dazed and afraid in the dark streets, pointing and marveling at the blackness of the morning sky. A foul storm! An angry wind, they say. There are some who scurry to hide behind closed doors and shuttered windows, some who climb the high rooftops and slanted balconies to peer at the billowing sky. Even the golden-sashed guards who still remain stare warily skyward from their posts. Some drift from their calling and vanish away into the wandering crowds, becoming another pale face to the sky. Too confused, too astonished and afraid to remain noble.

There's no one standing guard at the western edge of the House. No one to stop him from creeping into his father's tomb. A place that might have been home to him once, long ago. The path is all blackness, but it hasn't changed. And the memory of it plays like the steps of an old dance at his feet. Right, then straight on for three openings—a door to the right and a corridor to the left. Then another door on the right. Left at the next corner. Up the stairs with the sunken stone at their middle, and a sharp right—into the cramped, almost entirely hidden passage that emerges beneath the West Stair of the Hall of High Hands. And then he stops. Then he is still. He, and all the air with him. Silent. Soundless, in the Hall that once brimmed with morning routines, regal voices, and noble strides—the hopes of a nation, carried on long-robed shoulders, in this Hall. But now all is still. And the sun-deprived morning can do little to light the scene from slotted windows high in the crown of the vaulted ceiling.

Now the son of Távihn is here, waiting for something in the air, *anything* at all, to tell him it was all worth it. That somehow, it was right to return to Tekéhldeth—that there was some purpose, some deeper design for him in this strange and terrible place—that his probable end will somehow make things better for the people. Or at least spare a few others from the same fate. But there's no certainty. Only the faint shimmering of hope that now burns in his heart—an unwavering pulse that no degree of sorrow or pain or regret could ever extinguish. And for now, perhaps that is enough.

Ten for one, or one for ten, they said. They'll be killed at the next daybreak. And now the One will walk into death with almost no plan at all. He breathes, listening to the calm rhythm of his own heart. The Angel still stands at the southern steps of the House. Perhaps in time, she will stop the monster that's risen in the shocked and darkened remains of the Golden City. But the ten who stand bound at the north wall can't afford to wait and see. Not anymore.

He walks directly up the center of the wide Stair, when he moves at last, mildly attempting to deaden the sound of his sandals on the cold stone. All the doors of the wide passage beyond the upper landing are closed snugly in their frames, when he comes to them. They line the broad corridor like soldiers at attention, guarding the way to the great scarlet doors that lie directly ahead. The doors he often heaved open as a child. He had learned to hang with all his weight on one bronzy handle, pulling steadily until the massive hinge would give at last and allow a gap just wide enough for a small boy to slip through over the threshold. He would often find his father behind those doors. Sometimes reading near the window, bent over rolls and rolls of records at his desk, or simply standing by the columns, watching the shifting shades in the afternoon sky with a faraway light in his eyes. Thehlýnin ran out through those massive doors the night his father died. Today he will pass through them again, perhaps for the last time. But the calm remains in his heart. And it surprises him. There's little time to ponder why.

At the end of the hall, the scarlet doors burst suddenly open, sending a thunderous clamor echoing throughout wide corridors of the House. A tunnel of roaring, glowing flames comes spiraling and lapping along the walls, the floor, the ceiling—clawing but not scorching the stone and wood there. But the heat is real. The hot gust rolls down the corridor and hits Thehlýnin like a great simmering wave, shocking the breath at his lips and gusting the hair from his forehead. The light of it all is dazzling and blinding, after so long in the darkness of the city. And at the center of the blaze, standing in the threshold, is the man Thehlýnin long hoped he would never see again. The man who always stands with a clenched fist and a horrible grin on his now-fiery face. The self-proclaimed King of all East Ataran, Sekýnteo the Golden. The glare in his eyes is a terrible shining, and the flames that follow him paint brilliant reflections on the polished floor.

"Come at last!" he exclaims, and his hands rise up in the air before him, his image wavering behind the heat that ripples there. "Come at last to be consumed as an offering to the flames! A wretched prize, in exchange for the traitors who wait beside their graves at the north wall!"

At the top of the steps, Thehlýnin remains motionless, fighting with all his will to remain in place.

Then the king pauses, looking sideways at the boy down the hall, as if some new thought has come to his demonic mind. And a twist comes to the edges of his wicked smile.

"No," he says. "Not flames, no. My *hands*. I must feel your death in my hands!" And with that he comes swiftly forward, crossing almost the full length of the corridor in a few great strides, coming so near that the flames begin to nip and sting at Thehlýnin's shoulders. The son of Távihn stands still, awaiting whatever end will come to him now.

But it doesn't come. Not yet. As suddenly as he appeared, the demon stops with fists trembling in the steaming air before him, a single step away. Stops with terror suddenly springing up in his wild eyes. And his flames retreat into a billowing red wall at his back. But why?

Alive! Still alive!

Thehlýnin breathes, still unmoved from his place. Something else has entered the corridor. He can feel it before he sees it. It starts as a calm, white glow at his feet, then magnifies to fill the hall, until the fire of Sekýnteo is rivaled—if not outshone—for brilliance. She has come. The Angel has come. She appears like the morning, somewhere behind the place where Thehlýnin stands—lighting all the House with her glow. She walks slowly past him, toward the man who stands in the flames. The man who shrinks backward at an equal pace.

"When will you stop this, my brother? How could you do this, with all the gifts you were given?" She speaks, and Thehlýnin is astonished at the softness, the tenderness of her voice. A voice like gentle bells on an afternoon breeze.

"I do not answer to you! You are no goddess!" Sekýnteo snarls hoarsely, his glowing face wrinkled into a terrible, furious mask.

"Only one whom she has sent," Faliéhl's voice comes as a cool and whispering breath against the scorching. "I gave you three days."

Sekýnteo gives only a sharp growl in response. He has backed almost into the threshold of the scarlet doors. The woman raises a hand out from her side as she walks, as if to direct his attention to the vast multitudes of souls that live and move without the stone walls of the House.

"What more would you do to these children? Tear away what life they have left?"

"I AM THEIR GOD!" Sekýnteo screams, and the sound of it sends dizzying reverberations into Thehlýnin's ears. "They are *mine*, and I will burn them as I please! You've no more power than I. You cannot save them!"

Faliéhl is weeping now. She shakes her head mildly, the way a heartbroken mother might shake her head at a hopelessly wayward child. But her eyes don't leave him.

"No, my brother. I cannot save them from their already broken hearts. I cannot undo the wounds you have given," she whispers. "But there is still hope for peace. There is healing." She's still walking—stepping with the grace of a queen from some heavenly realm, coming ever nearer to the demon king who rants in the red embrace of his living fires. He lets out another furious cry, releasing a new burst of flames that radiates out from his person in all directions, sliding and licking along the empty walls.

"There will be none left to save! I will destroy them! And all that remain in the world will live to worship my glory!" he screams, and he raises his fists in the air. A violent quake rips through the stone floor, hurling Thehlýnin against the wall at his right and nearly knocking him down the steps to the open Hall below. But the Angel is unshaken.

"I cannot save them as they are," she says—her voice now loud and stern above the quaking, "but I will give them hope. There are those who will remain. They will overcome the blackness you brought to this land."

What happens then is almost a blur to the son of Távihn. The blended voices of rumbling earth and shifting stone, the rasping hiss of flames ballooning and bursting from their bounds—all cloaked in the wild contrast of white and yellow light that streams from the two beings who stand in the midst, human or otherworldly, real or unreal. All framing the sight of the Angel rushing suddenly forward—a shining, crystal blade clutched in her hand. And her final shout is a song that resonates far beyond the moaning of the massive bricks of the House.

"I will give them new life!"

The blade slides swiftly from her hand and vanishes into the king's fiery heart, unlocking a piercing, horrific cry from his chest—a shriek that seizes the hearts of all who hear, from the eastern hills to the western river docks. And the world begins to quake. All the city is trembling now, threatening to collapse and crush any who stand within its borders. But Thehlýnin is still alive. Breathing deep, marveling too much to make any satisfactory explanation in his mind. And so he stops trying.

Run! Escape!

The idea comes sharply to his thoughts, and he finds himself shuffling to his feet. Northeast! A northeast path would be best. There's less city to run through to the north. And the others! He must find them! The western alleys will be too treacherous a path for them now. They must go northeast!

He rises and turns to grasp the curving handrail of the West Stair, to find his escape from the tomb that was once the House of Voices. But there's something in the way. Some*one*. The girl from the house in the outer lanes stands at the top step, brown eyes wide and glossy, windswept curls drawing loose arcs across her pale cheeks. There's no time to ask, no time to wonder how long she's watched there, no time to say anything at all. There's only time to escape. They run together. They run as well as they can toward the eastern halls of the House, while the world heaves and reels all around them—to the place where the open court allows a sweeping view of the Grand Way between the columns. And the view is like a terrible dream.

Beyond the marble walls, the great torches of the Way have toppled from their high thrones, pouring out their fiery keep and sending their flames spewing and leaping into the streets and alleyways. The earth continues to rant beneath the foundations of the city, and the high towers have begun to teeter in their places—swaying from side to side as if to wave away the blackness that's settling like slick fog over all the land. The people run like helpless, frightened animals in the streets, shrieking and shouting as they go—and all the while the horrible cry of Kyvóike Sekýnteo rings out with dreadful piercing in the dark air.

The girl pauses between the columns, staring at the scene of it all, and the tears are suddenly cascading down her face.

"Mother!" she gasps, and she moves before Thehlýnin can reach to catch her wrist—darts out over the steps into the shadows and screams and chaos.

"*NO! LORËU!*" he cries desperately, reaching fruitlessly after her. But she is gone.

41

There's a slow throbbing in my head when I find myself again. Deep and rhythmic. The weary echo of my heart in my veins. The subtle witness of blood and breath that this little body still lives. Beyond it, I hear nothing at all. It's so dark. And the stone is so cold, so unforgiving beneath me. It's stone. Not sharp and crumbling but smooth and even. Polished. It was night when we were talking—night in the canyon as Thayl and I walked—night when . . .

I try to focus, try to find outlines in the black air before me, in the shadows that have closed in all around. So dark and silent. So unnervingly silent. I wait. In time there's a soft light falling in between dark columns, gleaming faintly into my eyes. Pale, silver light. The light of the moons. But the stars can't be seen, not here. It was night in the canyon. But this isn't the southern cliffs. I raise my eyes. This is a place I've seen before. A place I've never cared to see again. A round, open study with raised, columned walls. An open study with nothing but the cracked and splintered remains of a massive wooden desk and chair to fill the empty space. The chair I once used to escape this place. The throbbing rises in my chest, despite my greatest effort to soothe it. Somehow I've come here, to this dark place—to this tomb I'd hoped to forget. Days, *weeks* of traveling—somehow all undone in a moment's confusion. And now I'm here, in the Citadel, at the heart of the ruins. It can't be, and yet it is.

I find my elbows, rise onto trembling knees. And then I spot my company. It stands motionless against the far wall—painted like a pale portrait in the chilled air, scarcely visible in the faded light. The figure

I once spotted in these dark halls, and again in the Avenue. The entity that haunted the camps of the men—that came first as a thick and terrible presence in this place, so many long months ago. I'm standing now, unable to free the scream that rises in my throat, with all my breath fighting at once for release.

Just escape! Just get away from here! Run!

My instinct chatters away at the front of my thoughts, urging me to move. But where is far enough? Even at the southern cliffs the darkness has found us, dragged me back to the tomb we woke in. Where could we ever hope to run?

Maybe running is pointless. But I have to try. A panicked shuffle is all I can manage. I move backward, kneeling clumsily to grab a long, splintered shard of wood as I go. My only defense. And I wish—wish with all the passion of my fainting heart—that I could find someone here. *Anyone*, to free me from this awful sentence. Anyone to save me from bearing this darkness alone. But there's no one.

I keep moving, shambling backward until I pass through the windowed passageway and find myself pressing my back to the towering red doors at the far end. I reach with my free hand, hoping desperately to grasp the handle, to push the massive door open. Such solid wood. Such massive, solid wood.

The entity comes down the hall then. Drifts after me like a puff of smoke in the shadows. I'm still pressing my back to the door, staring through the watery blur that's risen in my eyes, when the figure stops. It leaves the intricate mosaic patterns of the floor framed and untouched between us.

"Does it bring you sorrow, to see the ruin of my mighty kingdom? Even this the greatest of the High

Houses might have fallen entirely, had I not preserved it with the last of my strength."

The voice is thin and echoless, falling like a hiss at my ears. Like the voice that came to us in the canyon. The voice of a man. And until it comes again, I don't realize—don't dare to believe that it belongs to the terrible figure that stands before me. I press again at the door, swallowing the whimper in my throat.

"It was a dark day when the Golden City fell. When the walls were rent and the high towers broken." The figure turns as he speaks, and for an instant I can almost glimpse the swaying of magnificent robes at his side. I blink and look again. Somehow, the image is becoming clearer before my eyes—something less like smoke and more like an outline, a silhouette. More like the ghost of an actual man. And it terrifies me.

"You were there; don't you remember?" His whisper slides out again, and his drifting motion gives way to solid steps. I can see him now, a tall man with black eyes and a strong jaw. A man draped in the long and shimmering robes of a king. But the colors are dull and faded, like the colors in an old dream, half forgotten.

"She tried to save you, she did," he says. "Thought she could give you a new shape. A shape that could survive when the old one was broken and tattered." He nearly spits the last words, turning suddenly to pace again along the tiled floor before me. "Yes, yes, a new body. A body capable of marvelous things. You could even mimic the face of man, if you chose." And he pauses to catch me in his black gaze. "But you can never be of Man again. She may have saved your little lives, but she could not save your humanity. And now you roam like wild beasts in the land!" His voice climbs unexpectedly from a murmur to a cruel and rapid snarl, startling the silence of this dying place and destroying what little calm had formed in my nerves.

Why does he speak? What's he saying? And what does it mean? His words crash and tumble in my mind, wrenching concepts from the deepest places in my memory.

You were there . . . a new body . . . and she . . .

The phantom comes suddenly forward then, and I raise my arms impulsively over my face. But he keeps away, turning in another abrupt circle over the colored floor, trailing gray wisps at the hems of his robes. He begins again.

"She tried to take it all away," he sneers. "Hoped to reclaim the glory that was *my* natural right, the power born within *me* and none other, from the moment *I* was chosen as lord and judge over this land!" His voice has risen to an almost quaking volume now, and he stops in his place, sending his glare through my eyes and into the black bottom of my soul. When he speaks again, the words are a sharp and terrible whisper. "My city is laid to ruin, my people turned to beasts. Even *I* am reduced to wander as a ghost, taking sand as my hands, moving dirt to touch the physical world. It may have taken all the power I could muster to find you scampering among the southern lands, so far from my sanctuary, to drag you back to this grave—but *I* have not fallen!" Then he comes striding toward me without warning, black eyes burning, and the sight of it pulls my voice from its hiding place.

"*STAY AWAY!*" My scream rings out and floods the high ceilings, hiccupping back and landing again with an almost deafening volume. He stops an arm's length from my face; the ghost, the man, the king—stops just beyond my outstretched hand. And I see that there's only blackness in the ovals of his eyes.

And an awful, fiery rage that nearly shocks the life from my heart. My breath begins to come in gasps.

"I couldn't take him. But he's coming for you. And he will fall into my hands. Here, where my power still lives. You think you are strong," he scoffs, and I almost feel the prickling of his words on my skin. "You only have what strength you can steal."

I can see his focus turn away from me to some unseen effort. Then a strange sound begins to rise from the tiles. A subtle, grinding hiss. The sound of wind-driven dust. And now the man is gone. But in his place the dust of the floor is swirling, churning, colliding—shifting and piling until it towers over me. I swing the wood in my hands, swatting at the mass and sending sand in all directions. The grains begin to pelt my head, tumbling into my eyes and over my shoulders. I squint and stumble backward, pressing again to the door—but the door has moved, and then I'm flailing my arms, struggling not to tumble over the figure that stands in the threshold.

"Thayl!" I gasp.

It makes no sense at all. I don't know how he's come here from the southern cliffs, or how he's managed by his own strength to heave the red door from its resting place, but there's no time to wonder. He pulls me to my feet, and we turn to dash down the corridor without saying anything at all. But we don't take the old path. We dart without stopping, through the labyrinth. Leaping down broad stairways, passing arches and pillars and rows and rows of shadowed doors—running until the stale air blasts and roars in our faces. The Citadel is never-ending before us. But Thayl knows the way. We run through places I never knew still stood, places that reek of summers past, of old lives and forgotten memories. Forgotten, but not lost.

Running, running.

Somehow, images come to me as we run—wash up like drifting leaves at the shores of my mind. I wasn't running then, when I first came to these halls. It was long ago when I came. And I was so afraid that day, full of questions, full of hopes.

Running, running. . . .

I was so careful with my steps that day, so afraid of being found. So afraid of what might become of him, my friend who came here. We're running in darkness now, but I can still see it in my mind—the way the corridor was lit with such odd, golden light; the way his dark figure looked, outlined by the flames and white-yellow glow that painted the space beyond, when I stood behind him there in the wide hall. I followed him there. The boy with the dark hair and the sad eyes. And there was a woman—tall and shining, glorious. Like an angel, like a goddess. The woman from the eastern sea. Her eyes were so sorrowful, that day. So sorrowful, the day she came to our people, to our land. Sad because it couldn't be helped, because everything had gone too far, been broken too badly to be mended as it was. Sad because she couldn't save us all.

Thayl and I come to an open passageway now, where the towering windows have lost their glass, and the pale gleam of near-morning light can be seen as it falls over the Avenue.

The Avenue. I see it, and the memory of flames rushes into my head. Flames. A rolling, billowing blaze that blanketed the Way, swallowing up the inns and the shops and the broad balconies, licking at the heels of the people that shrieked and darted like frightened minnows in all directions. The fire that poured when the high torches fell. I ran through it, when the end came. Ran to meet my sister in the smoke and flame and flying ash. Ran to find our mother. But we couldn't find her. Streets and alleyways, narrow lanes—winding, endless cobbled paths before us, all flooded with figures. Running, stumbling, and terrified. Covering their ears against the roaring sound of dying towers. And the darkness was stifling. It lay thick on our eyes, stuck like cold silt on our skin. Cold, and suffocating. We couldn't find her. The maze never ended. It jolted and shuddered all around us, and I felt myself forgetting how I came there, where I was running to, who I was. We never found our mother, before the end.

The memories come like a sudden gust of cold wind, tossing my focus, blowing me nearly off my feet as I run. I stumble and throw out a hand to catch myself against the wall, blinking away the water in my eyes. Thayl comes to a stop just ahead. The long passage has ended. It opens to the ruins in a tall and magnificent archway, where the early morning air rises to meet our heaving lungs.

I'm too overwhelmed, at first—too flooded and confused by the memories that tumble in my mind, too thrilled at the thought of escaping this place, of escaping the dust and the darkness—altogether too distracted to truly see the men standing there, closing off the end of the hall before us. But I find my breath, and then I see them. And my heart takes a sickening leap in its place. Men. Nine—ten of them together, standing with their hands full of blades and clubs and pointed things.

"They must've seen me coming here," Thayl murmurs without turning his head. I come to a stop beside him, staring at the glinting blades in the men's hands, wondering if we could manage to slip past them, trying to ignore the cold, crawling sensation that creeps along my neck. We need to get away from this place. The ideas begin to whir in my head. We could run back—could leap from the windows, climb out where the men couldn't reach us, couldn't find us. But Thayl doesn't turn back. He opens his mouth and speaks. Not the words I've always heard—but other words. A kind of speech I once learned, a language I know I once spoke, long ago. It's old and strange to me, like words of a dream. But I remember now, and I understand them. The speech of the West. The speech of the men.

"There's no fighting the shadow of this land!" Thayl tells them, and his words leap and ripple back along the walls, fleeing into the dark corners of the Citadel. "Coming here will only endanger your people!"

The men are taken back at first, turning to glance at one another, shifting their weight from one foot to the other. And I hear them whispering.

"The demon speaks!"

Then one of them bellows back.

"How would you claim to know, devil?"

Something happens to Thayl then. He takes a step toward them, and I can see a kind of wild light in his eyes. There's a firmness like stone in his step, in the straight arc of his back, in the way his green sash hangs in dark folds along his shoulder. He becomes something greater, someone ancient and tragic and terribly familiar—and when he replies his voice falls like great stones in the air. Full of sorrow.

"I know because I was here when the darkness came," he tells them, and he raises his voice. "I know because I am the son of Távihn, the eighty-first Eviskyóneh, who fell by the blade of the eighty-second. The man who took my father's life lives on as a ghost to haunt this land. And he is more than a man. It was his rage that brought ruin to all the regions of East Ataran, and they are all lost. This is his grave, and his realm. I beg you to leave these lands, *please*—there's no destroying the force that dwells here. There's no stopping him. Not with all your weapons and armies."

Maybe the men are surprised, or maybe they're shaking their heads in shock and disbelief, some of them stepping away and dropping their clubs. But I don't notice. For this moment, I only notice Thayl. I watch him, and all the world seems to fade to silence around me, circling and funneling around this instant before me, around the truth that comes pouring down on my mind—a reality that's too terrible and too complicated to understand. The reality that was never really forgotten, in my heart. The truth I've always known. But there's no time to understand it, not now.

I see the dust coming before I can think to react—sliding past us along the floor, rising in a dense cloud before the men. Thayl sees it too. He leaps toward it, reaching to swat at the shape that forms there, the mass that positions itself to surge at the crowd. But the men don't understand, and one of them hefts a thick spear to aim at him. I move without thinking, slide beneath the lifted point and steal the strength from the massive arm that wields it. The man yelps, and the weapon comes clattering to the floor. And then I'm on my feet, screaming with all the breath in my lungs.

"RUN! Get out of here! Get away from this place!"

The mob turns in a storm of rattling buckles and heavy footfalls. They flee down the steps, beyond the archway and into the fading night. And we follow at their heels. I turn to glance back at Thayl, to assure myself that he follows. He's running, coming my way. But he doesn't come far. He's looking directly at me. I'm watching, when the cloud of sand rises behind him. I'm watching—helpless to turn back time, helpless to interrupt the nightmare that plays before my eyes— when the cloud pulls suddenly together into a narrow shaft, when it lurches swiftly forward and comes piercing through my beloved friend's chest, sending him shrinking to his knees. Then onto his hands.

I feel the breath escape my lungs, a shriek sliding out between my teeth. And I do all I can—kicking, swatting at the sandy mass, pulling Thayl from the steps where he's fallen. I fight with all the energy of my soul, weeping hopelessly as I beat the sandy beast into the ground. I stomp and trample it there, until the dust rises no more. And I command it to leave us.

Then there's such silence, in the ruins. There's only silence, as we stagger away into the shattered cobble paths. Only silence as we stumble and collapse at last among the broken bricks and stones and mortar, Thayl's life pouring out all over, hot and wet. I lay him down in the dust, try to wrap his sash against the bleeding—holding him carefully, sending all my strength into his heart through my chest and arms and the palms of my shaking hands. Somewhere far away, the sun has begun to rise beyond the tops of the hills. Now its light begins to swell and glow all around us. Thayl finds his voice. He stares past me as he talks, like he talks to the air or the sky.

"Maybe . . . maybe I never should have come back to Tekéhldeth." And a weary smile comes to his face. "But . . . I had to."

I shake my head.

"It was our fault that you stayed," I say. "My family insisted. We thought of you as one of our own." He lifts his dark hand, lays it over mine atop his heaving chest. He's looking at me now.

"I'm so grateful you did," he says.

"I should've sent you away," I tell him, and my voice begins to tremble beyond my control. "You could have lived all your days in the West, never knowing the sorrows of this place."

I remember him entirely now. I remember the boy with the dark hair and distant gaze in his eyes, the boy I found standing beneath the bridge that day, when the rain was misting the fields and pattering along the stones. The young man who came from the West with nothing but a fisherman's shawl to keep the cold away, who went alone to the throne of a demon king who swore to kill him. Thehlýnin, the one who was there in the end, who was there in the beginning. Thayl.

He shakes his head.

"No, no, Lorëu. It was meant to be this way. It was worth enduring—all this. For the sake of our people—a new people—who will live on." He brings his hand to my wet cheek. "It was worth seeing my people overcome their struggles. It was worth knowing you. I wouldn't want anything else." His breaths turn ragged, and I take his hand, try to will the life to remain there.

"Don't be afraid, Lorëu," he says. "Look for me."

His fingers fall loose against mine, and as I'm watching, I see something flicker in his half-open eyes. A faint glimmer of light, like the stars as they twinkle out at the coming of dawn. And then he is still.

I watch the wind play along his sleeping face, and a song comes back to me. A song from long ago, from another time, another life.

> *Red ribbons blowing*
> *Flying*
> *High and restless*
> *Beyond the tower*
> *Where the winds are cracked*

Against the city wall
Look for me
Where they hang—
Red ribbons blowing
Hopes long lost
But never forgotten
And come the haze
Of morning light
You'll find me waiting there.

The words begin to slip out on my breath, sliding like the wind over the ruins. Pouring softly from the open place in my heart. But I can't seem to find my voice for the second verse. And I can't see beyond the tears. And so I sit in silence and hold my friend, until the last warmth has gone from his broken body.

* * *

I'm standing in the middle of the Avenue, unsure how to hold myself, unsure of the world before my eyes, when he comes. The dust and old ash of the Grand Way swirls and flies all around me, but I hardly notice. I'm standing like a lost and hopeless child, when he finds me. And he says nothing at all. But he takes Thayl's lifeless body in his arms and turns toward the southern hills. And I follow him.

We bury my friend to the southeast of the city, just beyond the walls of the orchard, where a single massive stone rises from the hillside. There was a time, when I was dying, that I dreamed of climbing it. Now the effort would be nothing at all. But I don't have the heart. And so I just stand there, staring out at the rolling earth, the wide sky. Unable to hide the trembling in my knees, my hands. Beside me, Kéthreo extends his broad hand.

"Come," he whispers. "I'll go back with you. I don't want them to come again and find you alone."

I nod and take a step toward the south, but the tears well up again, and I'm stumbling blindly through the tall grass. I don't struggle when he stoops down to take me up in his long arms and carry me gently away. Carry me like a skinny little baby, in his strong arms.

All the days of my waking life, I've tried to remember. Now the memories come like cold rain into my mind—dropping their full weight on my fainting heart and pressing the breath from my chest. Now, I remember it all. The old scenes hang as murals in my mind. Paintings of a torn and faded life that's so far from us now . . . so far from us now.

* * *

I see Évrieth in a dream, when night comes again.

"You already knew, didn't you?" I ask her. But she doesn't answer. She only smiles, spinning slowly in her white dress, tucking her long curls behind one ear. She's always seemed different, when she comes to me in dreams. But now I recognize why. Now I can see that she's no longer covered in dark fur, no longer staring with such large and shining eyes. Now she's human. Like I used to be.

42

The sun has dwindled to a low place over the western mountains when I catch first sight of the others. They're almost an illusion at first—a subtle shifting of color in the shadow of the massive red boulder that rises so suddenly from the open land ahead. It's a wide, sharp-angled stone that reaches with boldness toward the sky, laying its orange and amber hues against the pale and windswept colors there. An infant mountain the shape of a perching bird. Our planned meeting point.

I hurry ahead for a better view, leaping here and there to avoid the ragged edges of the stones at my feet. Kéthreo is smiling when I turn back to him, walking with his thumbs tucked casually beneath the edges of his belt. As if the nineteen-day journey we've just completed was little more than an evening stroll.

"We've arrived," he says. His voice rings like such music to me when he speaks the words of the West.

I spot Lotánehl first, when I look ahead again—and I can't suppress an elated gasp. *My people! My home!* There was a moment when I might've lost them both. But not now. Not ever again.

Ahead, Lotánehl climbs atop a jagged boulder and shields his eyes, looking our way, then waves his arm high in the air. A welcome. I wave back, almost stumbling in my excitement. Then the gray boy slips out of sight. I've only walked a few paces more when he returns, a pale girl in a red sash following closely at his side.

"Ilith!" I shout, and suddenly we're running to meet each other in the flat plane that divides us, leaping stones, dodging shrubs, and swatting the swaying grasses. She catches me by the shoulders when she reaches me, looking me hastily over, then frames my weary head in her hands.

"*Linén tsitá*!" she gasps. "What relief! You have no idea how little I've slept, waiting for you! What kept you? Did the men find you?"

I shake my head.

"Something else did. Something far worse," I tell her, and my voice trembles. "But everything's okay. We've made it back." I begin to ramble, hoping to somehow talk around the gaping hole in my heart, but her puzzled expression interrupts me. She glances over my shoulder, then silently in all directions. Then back to me.

"Thayl?" she whispers.

I thought I long ago wept out all the tears in my body. I was wrong. I bite my lip, swallowing hard to push past the sob that rises in my throat. But my voice is trapped beneath it. I only shake my head. Ilith says nothing. Her emerald eyes widen, and she pulls me into her arms, tearing down what little resistance I had against the tears.

"We'll find him again," she murmurs softly, and her voice resonates in deep rhythms against my ear. In a way, her words make no sense to me. But they pull at something inside me—prying at some knowledge, some assurance that lies just outside my ability to grasp. The subtle assurance that we will all meet again someday, in another place. Perhaps at the place where Évrieth and the others are waiting. It's something I can't understand. Not yet. But I believe Ilith.

I know she's spotted Kéthreo when her arms loosen subtly around me. I turn to see him, leaving my tears in a rough smear along my sleeve.

"This is Kéthreo. He's not like the others. He brought me back," I tell Ilith. She gives me an anxious glance, then turns back to the man who comes walking to meet us. She's silent, fingering the vibrant hem of her sash as he crouches down beside us. And she stares at him with an intensity that few could endure. When she speaks at last, her first words are scarcely audible above the sweep of the wind along the plain.

"I remember now, that face. I used to see faces like that all the time."

Kéthreo smiles calmly in response, as if everything was entirely as he anticipated. I touch my hand to his broad shoulder.

"Will you stay with us, for a time?" I ask. His pale eyes turn to me, somehow full of light, despite the slow sinking of the sun. Full of warmth.

"Of course, if you wish," he says.

* * *

That night, Ilith and I talk until the twin moons are high in their midnight thrones. I tell her everything. We sit with our backs to the southern face of the Bird, looking out to the darkened, sleeping lands beyond. The others fell silent long ago. They sleep in little clusters along the base of the stone face, curled into the folds of each other's shawls and blankets. Behind Ilith, even Ekyán's eyes have drifted softly shut. And the glow of the stars lays an array of almost sapphire hues along the curves of his broad, webbed feet.

"Did you find it? The place Ekyán wanted to show you?" I ask, keeping my voice low. Ilith nods.

"Only a day's journey from the western bank," she tells me, and her wide eyes are suddenly gleaming. "Lorëu, I wish you had seen it! There was an entire village there. Still standing. In a grove where the trees and bushes have climbed all over the remains of the little houses. Their roots and vines looked like curling claws on the old doors and window frames." She raises her hands in the air between us, mimicking the shapes of the vines with her slender fingers. Watching her, I can almost see the scene playing out on her face. "*Our village,*" she says. "I remember it now. It was like my mind cracked open, when we found that place."

"Did you find . . . ?" I'm not sure how to ask. But Ilith understands. She nods, letting a soft breath slide out from her teeth.

"On the north end of the village. The whole house was covered with leaves and dust. There were only bones. But I knew our mother's blue dress, when I saw it. We . . . we buried them in a meadow nearby," she whispers, then pauses to look up at me with a delicate smile at her mouth. The kind of smile that comes with a hint of bitterness at the edges. "The wildflowers grew so tall there that the blossoms were tickling at our ears."

I listen, and her words press a soft wave of nostalgia into my mind. A memory of flowers—the pale red and violet blossoms that my own mother loved so much. The kind that grew along the back wall of our home every spring. And when the summer winds blew from the west, the blossoms always breathed such sweet perfume into our open windows. Mother. . . .

"So many lost," I murmur, swallowing the subtle quake in my voice. "I'm glad you still have Ekyán."

Ilith glances to the sleeping boy behind her.

"I never could have left without him. We were away from Shardehn, traveling in the north, when the darkness came. But I don't remember why. Not yet," she tells me.

"Shardehn?"

"The name of our region. One of the Ten. I remembered it when we started south again, the next morning."

Somewhere nearby, someone lets out a faint, mid-dream sigh. A sound made audible only by the rock face that echoes it back. I tip back my head to stare up the length of the stone. Its sharp edge cuts like a dull blade into the portrait of the night sky, jutting abruptly into the sea of silvery blackness that drifts there. The stone is like a shield at our backs—a towering door, closed against the fears and uncertainties of the lives we've lived until now.

"Even after all we're remembering, it's hard to believe we had an entire nation here," I say, and I shake my head. An entire nation that only exists in our minds now. How can it possibly fit?

"Everyone's beginning to remember now," Ilith whispers.

I glance over at Kéthreo, where he sleeps with his head propped slightly and his hands linked loosely over his stomach. So peaceful. When I turn back, Ilith's staring too.

"Was it strange, traveling all this way with him?" she asks, still watching him.

"I've never felt safer," I tell her.

"Why has he helped us?"

"He told me he wants to help us survive. Help us escape East Ataran," I explain. "It's strange: I remember now that we were like them. We lived our whole lives with bodies like theirs—only yesterday. But Mankind still seems so foreign to me. How can our heritage become something foreign to us?"

"Maybe we're meant to build a new heritage for ourselves. We've become something new," Ilith replies, leaning forward to rest her chin on her knees. I take a moment to close my eyes. They're beginning to feel heavy. Then she whispers.

"Do you think there'll be more of them?"

"More of what?" I ask.

"More people like the one who destroyed our nation," she says, not turning her sights from the distant night.

"Or like the one who saved it," I add, looking back to the grasses that quiver softly against the night wind. "I don't know. I suppose there may be, somewhere, someday. If those old tales were true at all."

"What do you think they were? Some kind of demons, come by some terrible fate to our land?"

I think for a moment, then shake my head. "I'm not sure. I'm not sure we'll ever know," I murmur. But the thought brings an interesting stirring to my mind. What was the name my Thayl had for them? *Sasariane.* What *were* they? Are there others? It was the unbounded rage of one of their kind that brought our land to ruin. And the gentle mercy of another that gave life to our race as we know it. What are they, truly? Maybe I'll never know, but something in me yearns to find the answer—to chase it down over sea and mountain, forest and plain, until I can capture it in my hands. Shepherds, judges, messengers—the old tales said. There must be a purpose for them to exist in the world. A purpose that they themselves are clearly free to reject. And how would they choose to wield their glory if they appeared again in some land? How could anyone hope to control the outcome?

Ilith sighs beside me, arms tucked into her sash.

"If we ever find another one of them, let's be sure the story of East Ataran isn't written a second time," she says.

"We will," I say. "We'll watch for them." And the sureness rises like a sudden warm tide in my heart. It would be worth all our efforts to save the world from enduring the sorrows we've already borne. The struggle our people alone were called to bear. If the Sasariane come to us again, we'll be waiting to receive them.

43

The others are finally beginning to feel more comfortable with Kéthreo when morning comes. Ilith, Lotánehl, and I return from the river's edge to find him encircled by a crowd of curious and inquiring little hands. Even sitting, his head is level with most of those that surround him—and taller than the rest. They study him with amazed whispers at their lips, reaching to touch his hair, his face, his shoulders and arms. He allows them to lay his broad hand out for inspection in the center of their circle, and all at once our brothers and sisters are reaching to compare it to their own, gasping at the differences they see there.

"*Vedo ji!* Such giant hands!"

"Look how strong!"

"Hands like this! I remember hands like this!"

Their voices ring out together in a playful chorus. Watching them, I feel a little swell bubbling up in my lungs—the fluttering edges of a laugh under my breath. It's a feeling I haven't had in ages. A feeling I've been starved to find again, from the time we buried the body of my best friend.

I set down the freshly filled water satchels I've carried. In the midst of his new fans, Kéthreo grins, apparently content to be poked and inspected. He looks to me.

"They talk about my strength," he says, using the words of the West, "but they could take it all from me in a single breath, if they chose."

"We only do that to men who throw spears at us," I say. Beside me, Ilith frees her hands before moving to crouch quietly at Kéthreo's side. I follow close behind.

"Lorëu told us of a place beyond the southeast shore. A place that would help us cross the sea to reach the eastern continent," she says, almost hovering off her knees. "Will you tell us more?"

Kéthreo looks over his shoulder, a kind of secret angle in the sharp line of his chin—like he might know everything in the world, if we would only ask the right questions.

"Just beyond the southeastern tip of the land," he says, and he snaps a twig from a shrub at his back, tearing away the prickly leaves to expose a bare point. We motion to the others, and they move away from the space at his feet. He draws loose shapes in the sand as he speaks—a large, uneven shape, then a series of smaller circles that lie in a sort of arching arrangement below the first. "If you follow the curve of the peninsula as it points to the east, I imagine you'll reach the first island by the evening of your first day. You'll be faster in the wind than our boats have ever been."

"A string of islands. And how many are there, before the opposite shore? Five?" Lotánehl speaks up as he taps his fist to his chin, staring intently at the map in the sand.

"Seven. They don't form a straight course, but this way you'll at least have resting points along the way," Kéthreo tells us, finishing the seventh circle. "The largest gap is between the seventh island and the eastern shore. Never sailed it myself. Neither have many others. But they say there are sailors who've crossed it in only two days, with less than favorable winds." I feel my lip pout as I consider the possibilities. Two days for boats. . . .

"If the islands have cliffs, there'll be updrafts we can ride," I say.

"Maybe we can learn to fly like the flocks of birds in the north, in angled formations. They must have a reason for flying that way," someone chimes through the crowd, and the others all begin to hum in approval, wondering softly to one another. Maybe we can do it. Maybe the eastern shore isn't far, and we could escape there. Maybe—

"Where do you think we should go when we reach the sea?"

The words are kicked up in my mind like dust on a dry road, stirred up by thoughts of the south, of the sea. They float back to me, rising up from some silent place in my heart. Framed in the voice I know so well. I turn from the crowd and shake my head, blinking away the cold water in my eyes. He won't be coming with us. Not this time.

* * *

We're gathered and ready to start southward again long before the sun has risen much above the rugged line of the eastern horizon. It's an oddly thrilling feeling to be moving together as a people again—a little flock of colorful faces, all full of wondering, full of simple dreams. Full of hope. But even as he helps us prepare, Kéthreo's gaze often turns northward.

I follow him to the plain beyond the north face of the Bird, near the boulder where Lotánehl stood the day before. Walking just outside his shadow, the way I've walked since the day we left the southern borders of Tekéhldeth. Now, it feels almost the same—as if we've just set out again on some long journey. But we haven't. And as much as I try to dispel it, the subtle wrenching only grows in my heart. Like a rope pulling tight.

I stop, staring at the sudden shock of colors that lie over the surrounding rocks in the morning light. I'm failing to hide the frown at my chin.

"What if you came with us?" I say. Ahead, Kéthreo pauses with his face tipped to the sky, closing one eye against the glare.

"It'd be hard to find wings big enough for this body," he says, and there's an unnameable gleam at the edge of his smile. What does he know?

"What if we made a boat?" It's an impossible idea. My human friend shakes his head.

"This is *your* journey, Lorëu. Yours, and your people's," he says.

"But, after all you've done . . ."

Now he turns back to kneel beside me, laying a broad hand atop my head. Near enough to send little puffs of breath over my shoulder. But he's becoming further from me now, slipping softly away as I watch hopelessly on. How can I stop it? I want to find some infallible proof, some sure reason why he needs to go with us to the East. But the answer escapes me.

Maybe Kéthreo can see the question in my face. For a moment, he stares back in silence, and I watch the subtle tremor of his long lashes as the wind passes over them. His voice is a whisper, when he speaks.

"I'm only as far as you imagine," he tells me. A promise. The words fall into my heart, tumbling into hidden places where only the dearest of hopes can remain.

Then he rises, turning to the north. I watch him go—until he's little more than a quivering shade among the distant stones and prairie grasses. And somehow, despite the gaping distance that blurs the edges of his figure, I know he's turned to wave goodbye.

44

I don't know how long I've sat here, watching the waves come in to shore. Hours, maybe. But I could watch for a few more. The waves are little, rolling and thinning out along the sand—reaching and reaching until their strength fails them, and they slide wearily back to sea. But they never stop reaching.

Out over the water, someone is practicing their slow turns. Rising on wavering wings, tail feathers twitching. I recognize the silhouette from my place among the rocks. He's grown some, but no one has such a tiny wingspan as Saiven. He was among the first to change, when we came here. We've camped near the southeastern shoreline for three months now. Yesterday the last five of our brothers and sisters awoke as virít. Now only three of us remain in our original shape.

A hand appears at my shoulder. I hadn't heard her coming over the voice of the sea, the wind.

"It's time, at last," Ilith tells me, and I can hear the relief in her voice. There's been something softer in her touch since she and Ekyán found the remains of their home in the southwestern woods. A kind of slow and solid melody that rings out from somewhere deep inside. The midmorning light leaps and dances over the distant waves, painting little stars in her eyes as she gazes out to sea. I breathe.

We've remembered so much since we came to the south shore. More than we could ever record. The memories came like dreams to us at first, faded and soft. But they solidified in time. And now when we open our thoughts, they begin to flood and tumble in like falling waters, expanding and magnifying and gathering momentum as they go. And there never was anything so marvelous to our minds.

All our days, we've wandered as strangers in our own land—stumbling blindly in the mist and fog that hid our memories there. But we learned. We found hitérian—the life energy of our new bodies, the key that allows us to change our bones and adapt our shape to the world around us. We learned to move it like fluid, like lightning in our veins. We've learned that the soul never truly forgets. That the truths we learn here are already remembered within us—and can be found in our very *nature*.

Now, we're recovering the lives once lost to us. We often wake to find that our names have come back to us, or the names of our families. We spend ages talking together, astonished by the memories of the streets we once walked, the songs we once sang, the dreams we once chased. We've begun to remember letters and books and stories told to us long ago, and the names only continue to pour—until we begin to name the mountain peaks, the rivers, the sea, and the stars in their slow dance. And it's wonderful beyond our ability to define.

Now, we're beginning to fill the gaps—to finish the once hopelessly stained and incomplete portraits in our hearts. We can recite to ourselves the precious details of a life we can no longer hope to live. But we don't need to live it, either. Not anymore.

There was a time when we were the people of East Ataran. There was a time when we pressed our hopes into the hands of men and women who rose like kings and queens in our high towers, and we lived by the direction of their voices. There was a time when one who might have lifted us higher only toppled the dreams we had built, and a time when the terror of his rule only destroyed the hopes we once carried. There was a time when we were human. But we don't need to be human anymore. This is our people. A young people—a new race that was saved from the ashes of the old. We are the *Voranjevin*, the "Overcomers." And we are all that remains of the Ten Regions of East Ataran.

"Sitting here, I sometimes hear the wind calling again," I murmur to the waves. "Calling us to the East." Beside me, Ilith is smirking now. She nods softly before she turns to catch me in her sparkling gaze.

"Then we'd better go to meet it," she says.

I rise to my feet. It's time. We'll find Ekyán and begin our change to virít together. We volunteered to be last. And when we wake, the others will be practiced and waiting. Kéthreo told us of the land beyond the sea. A land free of old nightmares, where old pains and fears are laid behind. Where a wandering people can begin anew. A new home. We'll fly there together.

I turn to glance again at the gray sea, wondering what world—what joy and sorrow—lies beyond it, wondering how we'll bear it all. But I'm not afraid. Not anymore. I know who I am. I know what it means to be Lorëu of Tekéhldeth.

I sigh. The wind is rising now, singing over the crests of the low hills, making the tall grasses dance and play all around us. And I can hear its song. The song I've always known.

And I'll never forget.

Have you enjoyed this book?

To give it your rating, write a review, submit a question to the author, or simply discover more information about the Ages of Claya series, please visit www.memoriesofclaya.com.

Thank you for reading!

Made in the USA
Middletown, DE
06 July 2017